EVIDENCE

of

GRACE

CANDACE ARMSTRONG

Paperback ISBN: 978-1-09833-595-3
eBook ISBN: 978-1-09833-596-0

Dedicated to my parents
Melvin Charles Williams
Edith Mae Williams

1

Born in a Train Wreck

The silver-grey minivan sped north on Sparrow Street. Charlie Jericho turned his head toward its roaring engine and jumped to his feet from his perch on his front steps, shaking and twisting his strong hands. His eyes darted to the railroad crossing beyond the scrubby field across the street and a few careless blocks from his house. The Norfolk Southern careened around the curve and accelerated only one hundred yards from the crossing. A horn blasted like the tooth-rattling scream of a dying animal.

The minivan hurtled along the street so fast it swayed sideways and caught the telephone pole on its left front fender while skidding around the corner on two wheels. Like a cartoon bumper car, it flattened the post of a stop sign and bounced onto the tracks coming to rest squarely in front of the oncoming train.

Squealing metal-on-metal brakes sounded, followed by a series of staccato-like crashes from the telescoping of fuel tankers into grain cars at the front of the train. Within moments, ethanol leaked from a ruptured tank and detonated, ignited by a spark from the hot steel rails. A massive fireball leapt far into the sky. The clangor assaulted Charlie's eardrums, and vibrations hammered with such force he thought they would shake his fillings loose. He drew back, gasping. Debris flew. A minivan hubcap rolled right over his foot.

Charlie screamed and ran inside to call 911. But there was no need. The explosion prompted a cacophony of sirens, already descending upon the scene. He swallowed hard before rushing toward the crash, until the reeking smoke rolled over him like a blanket, dropping him to his knees to crawl beneath it until intense heat pushed him back.

Firemen doused chemicals onto the strung out wreckage, and the minivan disappeared. A mean, acrid smell belched out of the heart of the wreck. Fumes spread in a thick haze over everything in the vicinity, burning Charlie's eyes and throat.

A baby cried. The sound drew Charlie toward a stand of uncut weeds closer to the accident site. The crying grew louder and more intense. A tiny shoe lay on the eroded gravel at the edge of Sparrow Street. Charlie picked it up. Now a kind of panic struck him and he crashed through the thigh-high weeds alone among the other people thronging the fringe of the accident scene. He found the baby in a waist high clump, still strapped into a carrier on its side.

Charlie turned the carrier over and fumbled with the bindings. One cheek was skinned by the rocks, but the crying stopped. He picked up the baby, hugged it to his chest. Standing there feeling helpless, Charlie shifted his weight from foot to foot, uncertain what to do. When the crying erupted again, he squeezed the infant more tightly, scooped up the carrier, turned and ran into his house.

"Too bad Mae isn't home," Charlie spoke aloud. "She'd know what to do; how to take care of you." He cleaned sooty pebbles from the baby's face as tenderly as he could with shaking hands, and he talked as he took off the singed, smoky sleeper. A girl.

"What do you eat, little one?" he whispered, swabbing her gently with a warm washcloth and wrapping her in a soft blanket. He found a small bottle saved from feeding a kid goat Mae had once rescued, filled it with milk and screwed on the nipple and collar. But she wouldn't take it. Charlie scratched his beard. *Of course. It's cold.*

Holding her while the bottle warmed, he closed blinds to shut out flashing lights and nearby carnage, but nothing could muffle the shouting, crying and incessant sirens. *Why don't they stop the damn sirens?*

Settling on the couch, he fed her warmed milk. She took it eagerly, and Charlie cooed to her big gray eyes, open and inquiring. After an awkward burp, she grew drowsy against his shoulder.

"Should I take you to the police now?" he whispered. "They might not believe me."

When Mae got home well after 3:00 a.m., they were both asleep on the couch.

Mae Jericho swatted back a few strands of her sweat-loosened hair toward her ponytail and pushed up the sleeves of her sweltering nurse's uniform. She worried about a young woman, pregnant, brought in from the grisly carnage with premature labor. The woman was barely younger than Mae and had the same caramel skin as Charlie. Threading her petite but forceful body through the injured throng clogging the hospital entryway, Mae pulled her out of line toward a makeshift exam room. A man holding a cloth to his bloody head cursed her.

The gratitude in the woman's eyes was unmistakable, but she stared at Mae in a strange way. Mae managed to take and record both her blood pressure and pulse rate before a contraction wracked her thin frame. Wrapping her in a blanket, Mae scanned the crowded scene of moaning and crying humanity with little hope of finding a doctor to attend this patient.

"I must find help," she said.

Before she hurried off, the woman whispered something Mae didn't understand.

"Ce soir, vous vas trouvez ton mieus be'ne'diction." She shrugged and the woman grasped her wrist and whispered with a heavy accent.

"Today you will find your greatest blessing." Mae broke away as the woman's eyes bored into her retreating back.

Mae slipped off her shoes in silence and dropped her purse on the upholstered chair with a soft thud. She bent over her sleeping husband, Charlie, to kiss his cheek and tell him she was finally home. An infant was nestled against his chest, and her hand fluttered to her mouth to stifle her sharp inhale. *Oh my. Why does he have a baby? Where did it come from?*

The street lamp cast a milky pallor into the darkened room. Mae was able to make out their forms but not their features until she leaned closer. Charlie's chin rested crookedly on his chest with his beard barely brushing the top of a small round head, hairless in that light. The gold in his wedding band glinted in opaque darkness against the baby's back.

Overworked and weary, Mae sunk to her knees and trembled. She touched the sleepers. Her husband's eyelids wavered, and the baby sighed. She stroked the baby's back with one finger; Charlie opened his eyes, then smiled.

Mae held out her hands, opened, to take the baby.

"Charlie?" she whispered, but he held his finger to his lips. Together they tiptoed into the kitchen.

By now, nearly 4:00 a.m., all but a few guards posted by the railroad to keep looters and curiosity seekers away were gone from the accident site. The quiet was expectant with questions. Charlie kissed Mae on the cheek and held her with the still sleeping baby between them.

"Charlie?"

"I rescued her, Mae. Be proud of me."

"A little girl?"

Charlie nodded. A warm, wet substance seeped onto the front of Mae's uniform.

"We could use a few diapers," he said.

Mae's eyes were shining. "And formula and bottles and baby powder and a crib and some clothes…"

"Now hold on, Mae." Charlie's voice was a soft alarm. "This is not our baby."

"Whose is she?"

"I don't know."

"Well, where did you get her then?" Her voice rose.

"Shh." Charlie took a deep breath and let it taper out. He reached across the table to close his still sleep-warmed hand over hers. "I told you I found her. When she was crying, all I could think of was helping."

"You what?"

"Guess you know about the train wreck?"

"Sure. Had to work four extra hours at the hospital and thread my way home through the back streets. Sparrow Street is closed. But

Charlie, what about…" Realization washed over her features as early daybreak spread through cracks in the kitchen blinds, giving the room a pale glow. "She's from the train wreck?" Mae put one hand over her mouth as if to stop her sudden awareness.

"It was unbelievable here, Mae. Those jolts from the crash and then the explosion made everything vibrate, probably for miles. Chaos, screaming, sirens. I ran right over there to help, but the heat kept me back, and then the police drove everybody away. I sat on the porch wringing my hands like an old lady, wishing there was something I could do." He hung his head.

"It was a nightmare at the hospital too, but Charlie…"

"I followed the cries over to that old weed patch across from Phillips' driveway. And there she was. One shoe off but strapped into a baby carrier. I brought her into the house to clean and comfort her before I took her to the police. You'd have to see her to believe me. But there was so much commotion, I waited until things calmed down a bit, and, I guess you saw, we both fell asleep."

"She's a miracle," Mae said.

"Yes, I'd say so." Charlie smiled down at the baby still sleeping in Mae's arms. "But she's not ours. We have to take her back. Someone will be searching for her."

"Maybe not. How do you know they won't think she got ground to pieces under those tons of mangled, twisted metal out there?"

"I don't. But Mae, she's not ours." Charlie closed his eyes. *Why didn't I think about what Mae would say?* "Wouldn't you have wanted me to take care of her?"

"Of course, you couldn't leave her there, but Charlie, she's our miracle, don't you see?" Mae grasped Charlie's hand and squeezed it.

"This is the answer to our prayers. Our little girl. Because you found her, it has to be so."

"Mae, we're talking about somebody's child here, not manna from heaven," he said. "We have to find her family."

Mae's eyes glistened. She lifted her chin. "She's already found her family."

Charlie made coffee in near silence, and Mae sat at the scratched Formica kitchen table, succumbing to a wakeful dream. Her mind recited a litany of items to care for a baby. The only sound was the baby's light sleep-breath until dawn crept upon the house, and the shouts of railroad investigators were heard. How would they answer a knock at the door?

Inhaling the aroma of the coffee for a moment, Charlie poured two cups and sat down. "Mae, whatever life she has, or had before the collision, she has people, somewhere." His shoulders slumped with defeat before his wife even spoke. There was no mistaking the spark of eagerness in Mae's bright eyes when the baby stirred and cried into the half-light of the morning.

Charlie yanked open the screen door while he struggled to hold two bags of groceries. The hinge popped out, and the door fell away from its frame. With great care, he set the grocery bags on the cement stoop and turned to push the door into place. *Shouldn't be too hard to fix this.* When he picked up the bags he smiled at a dozen bleached cotton diapers fluttering in the breezy sunshine on the clothesline.

Inside, he pulled a newspaper from one of the bags and carried it to Mae, who was sitting in his grandmother's old rocker holding the baby. Her skin glowed and soft contentment filled her face.

Charlie kissed the top of Mae's head, and pointed to the newspaper, mouthing "Read?" Mae nodded before carrying the tender bundle to the small crib they'd kept after Charlie had crafted it a few years earlier. The baby sighed and settled into the softness. Holding hands, Mae and Charlie crept into the kitchen.

Charlie poured two cups of coffee; Mae smoothed the newspaper over the top of the table. Her brow furrowed when she skimmed the front page. "Nothing here," she said.

With systematic concentration, Mae read each article on each page. Tucked into the lower left corner of page five she found it.

Ex-Mayor's Infant Granddaughter Missing after Vehicle-Train Crash

As a follow-up to our previous report of Monday's fatal vehicle crash with a Norfolk Southern on the Indiana line (see page A2, Tuesday's edition), the infant child of one of the victims is missing. Tillman Police Sgt. Lloyd Andrews stated today the body of Grace Gilliver Richards, the granddaughter of former Mayor, the late John Gilliver, has not been identified. She was believed to be a passenger in the vehicle at the time of the accident that killed her mother, Lisa Gilliver Richards, and a sibling, Benjamin Jack Richards, Jr. Anyone with information on Grace's whereabouts should contact the Tillman Police.

The explosion critically injured five, including two firefighters. One of the two firefighters, James Noble Jr., has been upgraded from critical to serious condition at Mercy Hospital. The other firefighter, Mike Sanders, remains in critical condition. Property damage estimates have not been released. The cause of the crash is still under investigation.

Charlie's eyes met Mae's over the steam from their rising coffee cups before they each looked away.

Charlie stared into the Formica. His thoughts tumbled in confusion, fighting to become the words he didn't have the courage to say. When their silence made him want to scream, he said, "Well, it sounds like Jimmy Noble is going to be all right."

A tear dripped onto the newsprint from Mae's lowered face. Charlie was gripped with fierce love and tender compassion for his childless wife. He reached for her hand then moved to hold her shoulders shaking with silent sobs.

When she quietened, Mae went to the counter for some tissue and busied herself with unloading grocery bags. She kept her back to Charlie as she spoke. "I told Crystal and the other nurses and aides on my shift that I'm taking care of my sister's baby – probably for a long time. They were all so happy for me, but Crystal asked why I'd never mentioned my sister. I said it hadn't come up, and now she needed me to take care of her little girl, Amy, until she gets better."

Charlie had been pretending to himself to read the newspaper, but his head shot up at her words. "Amy?"

"Yes," Mae said, still not looking at him. "I'm calling her Amy. I've always liked that name, and it seems to suit her." She smiled as she unpacked the formula. "What did you tell them down at Mercer's when they saw you buying formula and diapers?"

Now Charlie paled. "Well, we told the same lie. I told Mercer we'd be taking care of your sister's child for a while. He doesn't know you don't have a sister."

Mae turned her shining face to him.

"See, Charlie, it's meant to be. God wouldn't have let that little angel survive that horrible wreck to be found by somebody as kind as you for no reason."

Charlie shook his head. "I'm nobody. That child is from money, Mae. Besides, if you lost your child, wouldn't you want her back?" Instantly he regretted his words.

Mae spun around to stare out the kitchen window, twisting a strand of toast-brown hair with her index finger. "Yes," she whispered. "I do."

Charlie went to her, hugging her. "Sorry, sorry. I'm such a dope, Mae." He closed his eyes and spoke into space above her head. "You're the only good, truly good person I've ever known since Nana died. I'd never hurt you." He held her close counting her heartbeats. Her smothered sobs slowed, halted.

She pushed back avoiding his eyes. For a minute he was afraid she would leave him, his greatest fear. He urged his rising panic to stop.

"If that's true, you'll let me keep this baby, our baby now. It's meant to be. She has no parents but us. Oh, Charlie, we can give her so much love!"

Charlie sighed with fatigue and defeat. He always surrendered to Mae. He reasoned she must be right because she was more educated. But he feared losing her more than death.

Judith Branson gave her daughter a fancy name, Corey Mae Branson, then shortened it to Mae, and that is how her daughter was always known. Judith was a stranger to Mae, but that week when she rocked Amy in Charlie's grandmother's old horsehair rocking chair or fingered the yellowing doilies the old woman had crocheted, she pushed down a fierce longing that surprised her.

The sleeping baby yawned and stretched but didn't wake. Mae wanted to hug her tightly, breathing in sweet baby-powdered perspiration, and never let her go. She sat rocking and staring into a past that wouldn't be forgotten, like a hazy phantom lingering at the edges of her mind.

She had been old enough to walk. Her mother held her hand as they made their way through the store. She had been frightened by the crowd pulsing around her and cried. Two or three times her mother stooped to her side, told her to be quiet but didn't carry her.

They walked on and on. She could barely keep up. At last they stopped and her mother lifted her to a chair in a corner. Kneeling, she told Mae to be a good girl, wait for her there and she'd get a treat. Then Judith had hugged her and disappeared among the shoppers.

She had been glad to not be walking, but time grew; she worried. She looked up at every passing face for her mother. No one paid any attention to the quiet little girl. Soon she had to pee and was thirsty. If she wet her pants her mother would be mad when she got back, so she held it as long as she could. When she leaked onto the chair, Mae's shame added to her fear, and she crawled down to hide beneath a clothes rack.

Still, no one came to her; eventually she cried herself to sleep. When she awoke, the room was dark and all of the people were gone. Mae had seen her mother for the last time.

Amy stirred. *I'll never do that to you. No one will take you away from me.* Mae kissed her forehead leaving a wet spot on Amy's soft skin.

One question haunted Charlie. Why was that Norfolk Southern barreling around the curve so fast that day?

"You know, Mae, the trains are going faster through here since they put down the new track."

Her direct blue eyes grew pensive above the pot of onion soup she was stirring. The aroma suffused their kitchen with a pleasant hominess along with the sparkling windows and pots of thriving herbs on the windowsill. Her vision shifted outside to the scraggly field across the road and the tracks beyond. The air was still tinged with the cloying smell of burning brush and weeds and the gagging smoke. "Now that you've mentioned it, you're right."

"But there's something about that particular train. It was a huge freight pulling cars of grain and then flammables. Why did it also have passengers on board?"

Mae bit her lip. "There was talk at the hospital about that," she said. "It was pulling an illegal load and that's why it was speeding—to get out of town fast."

Mae and Charlie quarreled. A week had passed since the train wreck.

"We might be seen as heroes," Charlie said. "It's just an idea."

"And not a very good one." Mae stood and ran her fingers through her hair. "How could you, Charlie? How could you even think that?"

He glowered. "You'd be surprised what I can think."

"What's that supposed to mean?"

"Nothing. Nothing, Mae. We did the right thing to save her but keeping her is turning it into something wrong."

She didn't back down and stood with her hands on her hips. Neither spoke.

Charlie focused on the cracked green plastic tile on the kitchen wall. He grimaced. Baby Amy sat propped up between pillows in the

garage sale highchair they had bought. Her clear gray eyes found him, awakening the guilt of betrayal in him. She drooled from a toothless grin and pumped her arms as if to clap.

"There sweet girl," Mae whispered and blotted Amy's chin with a faded dishtowel. "You have to be pretty for Daddy."

At the word *daddy*, Charlie felt a gut-deep pang. *Is this what it takes to make her happy?* Already he was thinking of the baby as Amy, knowing from newspaper accounts read to him her name was Grace. The truth was colliding with the deception in their lives more acutely every day, just as the train had collided with the van. If he could no longer trust himself, how long until he could no longer trust Mae? How much longer until he forgets and accepts the lie as truth?

He smiled at Amy and seeing that, Mae smiled at him. She came to stand behind his chair, hugging his shoulders and kissing the top of his head. "She already loves you, Charlie," she said. "You are her true daddy, no matter who the biological father really is. You rescued her and brought her to me. Our little angel."

"She's everything you, we, always wanted. But I'm afraid to love her and unable not to. What if someone comes and takes her away? You know, a man like me..."

He pulled back and looked up at her, his brown eyes questioning.

Mae stroked his hair. "They won't, Charlie," she said. "God has given her to us, and it's up to us to figure out how to keep her. I know we can do it."

"It's more than that. How can I live with myself if we keep her?"

She soothed him, caressing his shoulders and arms. "It's okay honey. We're a family now."

Baby Amy chose that moment to begin wailing.

2

Loss

The sparkling clean window gave Sylvia Gilliver a view of the row of Black Haw viburnums that edged the immaculate property. Each creamy white blossom showcased its delicate green center at a perfect angle, creating the impression of a fence, a natural screen alongside the building to keep out prying eyes.

The Styrofoam cup of coffee she held steamed. Behind her, Mr. Willingham cleared his throat.

"Well, that's a problem, Miss Gilliver," he said in a low voice, respectful from years of practice. "Perhaps your niece's remains may never be identified."

"She was so small," Sylvia said, still regarding the mocking May sunshine. "Barely three months old, but still…"

"We have only two sets of remains at this time," the Funeral Director continued. "We will of course include your niece's memorial along with your sister's and nephew's, if that's what you want."

Sylvia faced Mr. Willingham. "No," she said. "I mean, yes." She sank onto a brown leather armchair across from a massive mahogany desk. "Mr. Willingham, I think there should be some remembrance of or for her, but without any evidence of her death, she might be alive, somewhere." Sylvia swallowed a sob.

"Take your time, Miss Gilliver," he said. "The service will be in three days, as we've discussed, and if you want to include your niece, we'll make sure she gets a proper memorial."

She looked up into the kind concern of his eyes. "Grace," Sylvia said. "Her name is, was, Grace."

They stood and together walked across the plush carpeting. He opened the door for her as she stepped into the formal, spotless foyer. There they shook hands. "I'll contact you tomorrow," she said.

Sylvia pushed through the heavy glass exit, glad to leave the cool sterility of the funeral home for the buzzing warmth of early summer.

"What do you think caused it?" Brian asked. His voice betrayed his usual control. "I mean, I've known Lisa longer than I've known you, and she's been headstrong and stubborn, but not reckless."

"I've been over this a thousand times to make sense of something that makes no sense," Sylvia said. She ran her long fingers through her streaked hair, pushing it back from the puffy redness of her swollen face. She pushed herself up from an elegant couch with a jerking motion, and crossed the room to an oversized picture window.

The view was of the river land below the hills where the house was tucked among its camouflage of trees. Lights were beginning to twinkle in Tillman, the town below the bluffs, as twilight rolled like a blanket over the early summer haze. Always the scene from this window had inspired or fascinated her. Now it seemed surreal, ironically cruel that life could go on.

She turned toward her fiancé, Brian, and encountered a brief déjà vu, but she suppressed it. He was often so unreadable to her. She frowned; then naked reality soaked her thoughts again. Tears spilled out, and Brian put his arms around her. The familiar scent of his Aramis aftershave was comforting.

"Maybe Jack was having an asthma attack," Sylvia said, "and Lisa was rushing him to the hospital. She must have seen the train coming; it usually slows by the crossing next to that cluster of old houses between the backwater and the tracks."

Sylvia broke away from Brian to sit in a wing chair across from the picture window. "Brian, they've only found two bodies, Lisa's and Jack's. No evidence of Grace."

"What?" Brian asked. The skin above his upper lip turned white. He gaped at her. "Are you telling me they still can't find the baby?" Shock settled around him.

Sylvia sputtered fresh tears, nodding.

"Well they have to," he whispered.

"How can they? They've tried."

"Not hard enough," Brian said, louder now. Anger contorted his patrician features. "What are they going to do about it?"

"It's more like what are we going to do. We have to make a decision about the service," she said.

"Damn it all to hell!" Brian stalked around the spacious room. "We can't just go out there and find her. You better tell them. What did you say when Sergeant Andrews told you? 'Well, okay?'"

Sylvia raised her voice too. "Why do we have to quarrel now, Brian? Sergeant Andrews was very kind."

Brian crossed his arms, still angry. "He doesn't get paid to be kind. He gets paid to do his job–like finding accident victims."

"Brian, I came straight here from meeting with Mr. Willingham at the funeral home. I can hardly function, and now you're yelling at me."

"Sorry, Sylvia. It's hard to put up with their incompetence, and I see it all the time." Brian knelt beside her, touching her arm. "I'm going to sue them. And the railroad. Why can't they find the baby?"

At that moment, the timers on the lamps in the oversized room switched on the lights. As if on cue, Marianna, the housekeeper, opened panel pocket doors that led to the dining room and stepped inside with a timid gesture, grasping her hands. She'd been crying too.

"Excuse me," she said. "I'm sorry to disturb you, but do you want something to eat? It's getting late."

Brian hopped up. "No. Only a drink, Marianna." Looking at Sylvia he said, "Better make that two."

Raw and defeated, Sylvia glared at him. Marianna left the room before she spoke again. "You're acting like Grace is our baby, Brian." She wanted to control her tears but wept with involuntary abandon once more.

Brian turned to stare out the window at the lights of the town and at the river below.

Why did Lisa die before me? Sylvia pushed her glasses to the top of her head, rested her chin in her hands and gazed into the dressing room mirror. Her fine hair separated to allow her ears to peek through, as it always did. Lisa's hair had been thick, dark and straight.

She saw beyond the thin-lipped woman in the mirror to an earlier time. Lisa, the princess in her ballet tutu, twirling around for her parents and their friends. That lover of the spotlight, although only two years older than Sylvia, had raked in admiration and affection with no effort.

The reflection was of her sister's eyes. The one good feature Sylvia thought she had was merely a replica of Lisa's.

"Why did you leave me?" Sylvia whispered to the mirror.

No answer, but a soberness in her large grey eyes clouded her vision.

"You were the favored one; you know that, you've always known that. I was supposed to be the boy. You were the outgoing, beautiful one and I was shy, even alone with you. You expected me to follow you and I did or at least I tried. It didn't bother you that I didn't measure up, but it mattered to them, Mom and Dad."

In her mind's eye, Sylvia pictured a younger self, overhearing her parents argue. The memory was so clear she could smell the roast beef they'd had for supper that night.

"There's no way she can make the grades," John Gilliver had said.

"But, she has to have the same chance as her sister."

"Think about the Gilliver name, Ruth. We have a reputation at Vanderbilt. They'll probably admit her because of my contributions and Lisa's academic performance, but it'll be an embarrassment to us and to the school."

"How can you talk that way about your own daughter? She's wonderfully artistic. She deserves the opportunity."

"Find somewhere else for her. If she insists on going there, which she probably will because her sister went, I'll have to sit her down for a frank discussion."

"John, don't you dare hurt her feelings."

Sylvia tore her eyes away from her own image in the mirror. Now they were all gone. She plucked a tissue from the dresser for her tears but balled it into a fist. "Well, big sister," she said aloud. "Now you've gone somewhere I don't want to follow. At least not now."

Brian Boggs sat at his polished wooden desk. Gold embossed scroll-work trimmed the leather inset. It matched the scripted gold lettering on the law books perfectly lined up in floor to ceiling bookcases behind him. In front of him were two ample leather chairs with gold-colored grommets at the seams.

Beyond the sniveling woman sitting there was a mid-summer river scene from his office window, which was also stamped with gold trim in the corners giving it a picture frame-like embellishment. Brian's clean-shaven face was free of expression, a practiced pose that allowed him to mask his thoughts from clients and in the courtroom. A new pine-musk aftershave wafted around him.

The woman stopped talking every few words to dab her eyes with a tissue or to blow her nose. On the elegant side table between the two chairs, she had amassed a small pile of used tissues, which he found disgusting. From time to time he feigned interest in her story by giving her a brief nod or an encouraging gesture. In truth he found it tedious and boring. He only half listened. None of his clients knew about the hidden tape recorder he always used to capture their wearisome and often long-winded details. Later he would have to listen to the drivel, but at least he could fast-forward through emotional interruptions. *And people think being an attorney is easy.*

The woman dressed up for the meeting, but tennis shoes ruined the effect of the tailored skirt and matching blouse. She carried one of those huge tote-style purses that didn't match her clothes. It now sat on the floor next to her containing a seemingly endless supply of fresh tissues.

"So you see, Mr. Boggs," she said after several minutes of describing her desperate state.

"Mike is only getting two-thirds of his part-time salary from worker's compensation, and the firefighter's union says they are running out of benefits. But like I said, our baby's sick too. My Mike's not home from the hospital, and he won't be working for a God-awful long time. I heard Jimmy Noble's wife hired an attorney over in, where was it? Cartersville, I think."

Brian's eyes flashed with involuntary emotion, the first he had permitted during this long interview.

The woman, Donna Sanders, didn't miss the slip in his façade. "Of course," she said, squinting her reddened eyes at him, "we knew she wouldn't contact you, but that doesn't mean we can't use a more convenient lawyer."

Brian flinched. *A more convenient lawyer. One with no potential conflict of interest?* He made a show of straightening the few papers in front of him. "Yes, well, Mrs. Sanders, I believe I have the preliminary information I need to make inquiries on your husband's behalf."

"Make inquiries?" Donna started a fresh round of tears, reaching for more tissue. "More than that, Mr. Boggs. We need a lawsuit. To get them to pay money. Mike would still be able to work if that train hadn't hit that car. So, it's their fault." She paused to blow her nose. "Besides, we heard you have some connection to that poor woman and her children who got killed in the crash. We thought you'd be looking out for their family and could just as well include us."

"Mrs. Sanders, let me remind you that a lawsuit may take some time to resolve," he said. "Years in fact. Also, there's the matter of my fee. For plaintiff's work, I'd get one-third of any settlement. Off the top."

"When we get paid, you'll get your money," Donna said.

Huh. The money goes through me and I take my share before you get yours!

Brian rose and guided her to the door. She stared at him in a way that made him feel uncomfortable. Closing the door after her, he swept the pile of used tissues into a wastebasket with one motion.

Some connection indeed.

Sylvia was supposed to be putting final touches on her trousseau. It was an old-fashioned concept, but she found comfort in clinging to some tradition now that her sister was gone.

Marianna had prepared a light lunch of petite toasts, fruit and tea for her, but she had little appetite, only sipping her honeyed chamomile. She inhaled its calming scent and let herself be mesmerized by the bluest summer sky, willing her spirit to fly away. Sylvia lacked enthusiasm for making wedding preparations and dreaded seeing her fiancé. Something was different about him since the accident, but she couldn't define it.

She called to her housekeeper. "Marianna, I'm going out."

Marianna frowned. "Yes, ma'am, but you wanted me to remind you about choosing the centerpieces. They have to be ordered soon to get them in time for the wedding."

Sylvia's laugh masked the defiance she felt. Marianna had taken to subtle nagging, mindful of her place but sounding eerily like Sylvia's mother.

"Okay. I'll order them. Thanks."

Marianna nodded and cleared away the untouched lunch, still frowning. "Will Mr. Brian be here for supper then?" she asked.

Sylvia's stomach jumped. "I don't know," she said as she breezed out. "I may not be here either," she called back.

Where could they have been? Sylvia drove south across town toward the railroad tracks below the hill. Near the scene of the accident, she parked in front of a small local grocery store, Mercer's, and got out. It was a fine, bright day with a summer scent on the breeze. An uninformed passerby would never recognize it as the horrendous crash site it had been only weeks earlier. But the clean wood of the stop sign and the stubble of renewing earth on long, bare patches of scorched and flattened weeds and grass next to new rails were all too obvious to her.

Across the tracks beyond Sparrow Street lay the narrow highway that led to her family's river cabin. Sylvia realized with a jolt it belonged to her now. Everyone else had died. Except maybe Grace. Or maybe not. She yielded to an awkward slump as if the weight of the whole incident pressed upon her shoulders.

An old-fashioned bell tinkled signaling the opening of Mercer's front door, and Sylvia straightened as she turned toward the sound. A bearded man with tightly curled hair and gentle features exited grasping a grocery bag in each arm. He smiled at her and in an instant she took in the frayed edges on the collar of his shirt, neatly tucked into his jeans, clean and pressed with shiny worn places at the knees. He nodded to her and strode past, erect and whistling. *Whistling. I haven't heard anyone whistling in a long time.* A happy tune.

Sylvia got into her Lexus and turned on the air. She frowned into the rear view mirror. *I should be happy too. My wedding day is only two months away.*

She pulled out and slowed the car to a roll as it crossed over the tracks. Blinking, she refused tears and turned right onto Sparrow Street, which became the road to the river cabin. Slowly accelerating, she passed the whistling man with the grocery bags walking toward one in a cluster of tired houses across from the railroad tracks. A clothes-line sagging with diapers bright in the sunshine peeked from behind that house, making a sharp contrast to the green shabbiness of its Enselbrook siding. Sylvia sighed and drove on.

Crossing the river Sylvia turned left onto a road flanked by dense woods then soon onto a gravel driveway leading to the cabin. The spare key was not in its customary hiding place under the false bottom of the mailbox, anchored to a porch roof post next to the back door. For a moment she panicked but then noticed the thriving weed-less flower-beds on either side of the back entryway and the fresh smell of clipped grass. It had always seemed odd to her to have a flower garden at the back of the house but it faced the road, and the spacious cabin with its generous screened porch faced the river. *The caretaker must have it.*

She saw dust motes dancing in the sunlight filtered through unwashed windows when she stepped inside the unlocked door. Everything seemed to be in order but was covered with a fine layer of dust. The bright daylight through the opened door highlighted the cobwebs clinging to the chair and table legs in the kitchen.

Her eyes were drawn to a shelf over the counter next to the door-way where Lisa always left the key when they came here. She, herself, would fling the key on the table or counter and have to search for it when it was time to leave. Approaching the shelf, Sylvia felt her heart skip when she saw the cabin key. Lisa was here before the accident. Sylvia sucked in her breath. A clean imprint of the key lay next to it on the shelf. *Someone has moved it!*

Turning to scan for any other signs, she wrapped her arms together—suddenly chilled. Moving with caution, she entered every room and searched for anything that had belonged to them—her sister or the children. Nothing but floating dust and slender cobwebs greeted her. Everything was in place.

Sylvia relaxed a bit and returned to the kitchen. Passing through the fireplace room, a flash of color caught her eye. Beneath the coffee table, obscured by shadow, she found a baby's pacifier. Grace! Tears filled her eyes. Yes, they had been here. She could almost see them.

"Ten!" Jack's chubby fingers covered his closed eyes. His shout was triumphant. "Here I come, ready or not."

He jumped and bolted from the room on his sturdy four-year-old legs. Hide-and-go-seek was now his favorite game at the riverfront cabin, especially since he had learned to count all the way to ten.

He searched for his mommy everywhere in the rustic but sprawling cabin. He looked under the twig chairs in the fireplace room, then ran onto the screened porch to check beneath wicker chairs and couch. Still no mommy.

His face puckered as he ran from room to room calling for her. Soon he was crying. Catching the edge of a floor rug, he tumbled onto his stomach, now wailing and sobbing in earnest. No one came to pick him up or comfort him. He calmed himself slightly, and then scrambled to his feet to run back into the room where he started. He saw his sleeping sister strapped into a baby carrier where their mother had left her. Putting a finger over his lips, he said, "Don't wake baby," in a hoarse whisper.

Looking around he didn't see his mommy and clattered from the room, panic rising in him again.

Jack's cheeks reddened and he gasped for air between sobs. Running through the kitchen, he stopped short at the screen door. He should not go out that door. It was a no-no, so he collapsed in a defeated heap on the threshold. On the other side of the screen, there she was. He slammed through the screen door, wailing for her. She was leaning against a car talking with a strange man.

Lisa Richards spun toward the sound of Jack's wailing and saw him trip on a sidewalk crack and fall. She laughed and rushed toward him, arms outstretched. "Silly boy. Mommy's right here." He was not bouncing up, as she had grown used to seeing her little boy do. She ran.

Jack's eyes were wide and dilated and his lips turned blue. He struggled to breathe.

"Oh, my God." Lisa scooped him into her arms. "He's having an asthma attack," she said to the man now standing beside her. He gathered the boy into his arms and ran back to his car.

Lisa screamed. "No! I have to get him to the hospital in my van. We can't be seen in your car. Take him to my van. There's an inhaler…" She was running alongside the man but suddenly turned and bolted toward the house, yelling. "The baby! I have to get the baby!"

The man strapped the boy into the passenger seat and held the inhaler to his mouth. Jack was gasping loudly when Lisa jumped behind the wheel, started the motor and thrust it into reverse. The tires kicked up gravel as the van fish-tailed onto the hard road at the end of the driveway and charged off.

Brian stood there, helpless.

3

Recollection

Jimmy Noble's father, James, sat at a gray plastic table in the hospital coffee shop talking to Jimmy's wife.

"The truth is, Nora, it's the third time Jimmy has cheated death," James said. "That boy is like a cat with nine lives." He slurped his coffee, then took a hearty chomp on a cheese Danish.

Nora looked down at her coffee cup, inhaled the pungent steam and raised her eyes to her father-in-law. "He won't be able to work for a long time, but…" Nora's voice broke.

James finished off the Danish in two bites as he studied her across the table.

"Well, of course, I know about the hunting accident last year. Jimmy was thrilled to be invited to hunt with those rich guys. He thought it would be a way for him to get to know them, maybe get a better job out of it." Nora sipped her coffee. "He's smart enough and brave enough to be a firefighter but, you know, he wanted to make more money."

The memory of the incident at Cedar Woods was still fresh but the pain of almost losing his son, then hearing accusations and going through the investigation was behind them. This time his son's injuries were heroic. No one could find fault with his actions.

Nora asked, "When was the other time? You said Jimmy had cheated death three times."

James began to pick up another Danish but stopped himself. "Jimmy had a buddy, Charlie Jericho, from work. At the woodworking shop."

Nora nodded. "Jimmy said he worked there once but then went silent. I didn't think anything of it."

"Those guys were thick," James said, swirling his remaining coffee. "Charlie's a great carpenter. He helped Jimmy build the cabinets for our kitchen remodeling, and they turned out beautiful. I've met him several times. Always liked the guy."

"Funny. Jimmy's never mentioned him."

"It was a long time ago, Nora. He probably wants to forget it. Want some more coffee?"

Nora shook her head, and James refilled his coffee cup before continuing.

"See, one of the fancy table saws had a short. There was a note on it–not to use–but Charlie disregarded it. He turned it on for some trim pieces for a special order. Then he went to answer the phone. Jimmy got to the saw first though and was shocked into unconsciousness. The owner of the shop performed CPR until the paramedics came and took Jimmy to the hospital. He was darn lucky to come out of it okay. They said his heart stopped for two minutes."

"I had no idea. What happened to Charlie?"

"He stomped around, threw down some pieces of wood, said it wasn't his fault, before he calmed down. The police investigator thought he'd done it on purpose at first, but nobody believed that, including Jimmy. Turns out Charlie couldn't read, and the shop owner didn't know it. So, he fired Charlie and no charges were ever filed."

"That must have been the end of their friendship too," Nora said.

James nodded. "Charlie came by to apologize, but Jimmy didn't want to talk to him. He didn't go back to work at the shop either. That's when he decided to become a firefighter."

"I accepted Jimmy's work was dangerous when I married him. Then, with that gunshot wound last year and all the newspaper articles and depositions with that awful attorney, Brian Boggs..." Nora's eyes grew moist. "But now this."

James drained his coffee cup. "Well, he's hurt pretty bad, but he'll pull through." He pushed his chair back and stood. "We'd better get back upstairs."

They rode the elevator in silence. Before the doors opened onto the ICU floor, James said, "I wouldn't mention anything to Jimmy about Charlie. It might upset him. I don't think he's ever forgiven Charlie."

Charlie never learned to drive. Old Mr. Phillips next door brought Lorraine home from the hospital in his battered pickup with Charlie riding in the back. She never left the house again.

Charlie did everything–in a cold panic. His sweet grandmother praised and blessed him and taught him what she could from her pillow-laden bed. But it was obvious she could do less and less.

She often talked about his mother, the beautiful Rachel. "Child, she loved you so much. You two were a picture together."

"If she loved me so much," Charlie asked, "why did she leave me?"

"Well now, remember she didn't just leave you. She left all of us, Charlie." Lorraine swiped an errant tear with the back of her hand. "Still wish I'd had the chance to give that girl a Christian burial."

"Where did she go, Nana? How do you know she died?" When he was younger, Charlie often entertained the idea of finding his mother someday, but as the years passed, a cold lump lodged in his gut. He'd never see her again.

"Because, sweet child, I know my daughter. She wouldn't leave you on her own. Or me either, for that fact."

Old Mr. Phillips looked in on Charlie and Lorraine from time to time. They didn't ask for help, but he could see Lorraine was bed-ridden and young Charlie took care of everything he could.

"Charlie," he said one day. "It's not right for you to stay here taking care of your Nana all the time. You need to learn how to make a living. Come with me to the hardware store."

Charlie loved using his hands to make things and especially to repair them. Soon, he was fixing squeaks in their wooden floors and adjusting old doors to hang right. He had a camaraderie with the wood, stroking and polishing it as he added the final touches. Old Phillips nodded appreciation at his attention to detail and began to rely more on Charlie's willing help with his own projects.

Lorraine and Old Mr. Phillips passed away within days of each other. After the simple services, Charlie was lost. Paul, the younger Mr.

Phillips, approached him. In the somberness of the season, Paul was unusually generous.

"Look man," he said. "My Dad would've wanted you to have his tools. I don't have any use for them."

Charlie's eyes brightened, but he swallowed hard and said nothing. He held his breath, afraid to exhale. It wasn't like Paul to be charitable, and Charlie didn't have money to buy them.

"Aw, hell, I could use the space."

So, Charlie became an independent carpenter, getting jobs by word of mouth because of the excellence of his work.

Mae found luck with her fourth foster home. Mr. and Mrs. Willis were experienced foster parents with a tried and true regimen. Mae thrived in their strict but kind environment. In high school, her curiosity was most aroused by Biology. She could never imagine anyone wanting to deliberately harm the magnificent creation of the body. She worked for Willis' brother-in-law at his hardware store during the summers in high school and after when she was training to be a nurse's aide. It helped to overcome her natural avoidance and fear of strangers when she had to talk to customers.

Mae couldn't help but notice an equally shy young man who came into the store often, usually with an old man who seemed to be showing him everything in the store. They walked through every aisle as the old man talked and talked, explaining what everything was used for and how to use it.

The young man had tightly curled brown hair, light tan skin and serious brown eyes. Mae shielded her own blue eyes when he looked at her, but peeked at him when she had the chance. Soon, the old man, a Mr. Phillips she knew from the checks he wrote, left them standing together while he went in search of one more thing. Shyly, they began to talk to each other.

"If you're a nurse," Charlie asked, "why are you working in this hardware store?"

"I said I'm a nursing student, silly. I'm working here for money to go to school." Mae giggled.

"Well, whatever the reason, I'm sure glad—"

They both jumped when a woman screamed. It sounded like it came from the back of the store. Charlie bolted in that direction. Mae ran after him.

In the paint section, a toddler had climbed to the top rung of a carelessly abandoned ladder swaying precariously as he reached for the uppermost row of cans. Without hesitation, Charlie ran up it.

The ladder clattered to the floor sideways as Charlie jumped down, the toddler in his arms. The woman rushed toward them and grabbed the child, crying.

"Thank God you saved him! Thank God!"

Everyone from the Store Manager to Old Mr. Phillips praised Charlie and shook his hand or clapped him on the back.

Mae alone said nothing, but her shining eyes belied her admiration.

Charlie had sensed her dreaming about him. When the days grew shorter, he chopped wood for winter warmth and wondered at the need because he felt hot with an unknown passion pulsing through his blood. By Christmas, they were married.

In spring, Mae blossomed along with the rebirth of the earth. Charlie relished the vision of her glowing skin and dancing blue eyes. After she came home from a long day, he rubbed her feet, and Mae basked in his love.

"Charlie, honey," she smiled at him and patted her stomach. "Did you know how much I want a baby? You've given me the one thing I've always wanted."

Charlie wanted their baby too, but he was also afraid. What if it turned out like him? He shook his head with steadfast resolve to banish the thought. The baby would be like Mae. Smart. He reassured himself every time fear crept into his mind.

Mae and Charlie moved through the lengthening days in a kind of trance, both feeling so blessed, so special. They saved every penny and talked about almost nothing but the baby. At the twentieth week, they eagerly arrived for their ultrasound examination.

"What name do you want for a girl?" Mae asked.

"I think Lorraine, after my grandmother," Charlie answered. "Or, maybe Rachel after my mother." Charlie furrowed his brow. "Not sure, honey. How do we know it will be a girl?"

"Well, we don't, silly. That's what we're going to find out today."

"If it's a boy, I like the name Jacob. He was famous in the Bible, Nana told me."

"I want to name a boy after you, Charlie. I mean, it would be so…"

Their conversation was interrupted by the technician who came into the ultrasound room.

She nodded and guided Mae to lie back onto the examining table. Soon, the grainy black and white image appeared on the screen before their anxious eyes. The technician explained the outline and movements of the shadows while gliding the instrument across Mae's abdomen. Everything seemed fine, then, abruptly, the technician stopped.

Charlie had heard her whispered "uh oh," but Mae had not. The technician stood to leave the room. "You'll have to talk to the doctor."

"What's this all about?" Mae said. "She just started the exam. Is it over? Now?"

Charlie clutched Mae's hand. An awful throbbing began in his head. "I don't know, honey," he said. "Guess we have to wait for the doctor."

In moments, the technician came back with a white-coated young doctor. They both hovered in front of the screen blocking Mae and Charlie's view. The young doctor turned around and took a deep breath. His hands were shaking.

"Mr. and Mrs. Jericho, is it? We'll need to talk to you before you leave the clinic today. So, please follow me."

"What's going on?" Mae and Charlie spoke together.

He sighed. "There's an, uh, irregularity. It would be much easier to discuss this in the office."

"Where's my regular doctor?" Mae asked. "I demand to see her. Why isn't she here today?"

The young doctor was halfway through the door. "Please, Mr. and Mrs. Jericho, just follow me now." He walked away. Charlie and Mae exchanged panicked looks.

"What does he mean irregularity?"

Charlie helped Mae down from the examining table. The technician held the door open for them and led them to a doctor's conference room.

"It's God's will," Charlie said. He sat with his arm across Mae's shoulders to tame his uncontainable heartbeat.

"I suppose, but I'm weary of his will," Mae said. She swiped her moist cheeks with the back of her hand. "If there is a God, He must know how much I want a baby. Why did this have to happen to me?"

"To us. We don't always know why."

"Yes, so I've heard. But I'm beginning to doubt. Seriously, Charlie. For a long time I didn't believe at all. Until I met you."

Charlie stroked Mae's hair and squeezed her more tightly.

"See, when I was in one of my foster homes, the third, no, no, the second. Anyway, they took me to church all the time. I was a good little girl, and I loved the spirit in the songs we sang. I was happy there."

"But then one time I was left alone in the children's room at the church for some reason. A man came in and held me against the wall. I struggled and turned my face away from him. I still remember the smell of cigarettes on his breath. I felt his erection pressed against my back, although I didn't know what it was at the time."

"What happened?" Charlie pressed his lips together. "What did he do?"

"Well, as it turned out, nothing, but I was so scared I was shaking. A woman came into the room, and he let me go. She hollered at me; asked me what I was doing. I ran out of the room and onto the front steps of the church. When my foster parents took me home, I told them I never wanted to go back. They forced me for a while, but I sat in the car when they went inside, even in the cold. It was one of the things they complained about when I was sent to another home."

Charlie was silent for a long time, hugging her close to him. "I don't think God had anything to do with that," he said.

"Well, he sure didn't stop it either and that man was a regular at that church." Mae pushed away from Charlie and stood up. "Anyway, that's when I started to doubt and even disbelieve." She cried. "Now that this has happened, he doesn't have any salvation for me."

Charlie stood too and wrapped his arms around her again. They both wept.

After recovery, Jimmy Noble walked with a slight limp, but he did everything he could do to disguise it. He considered it good fortune to be back on the force and was maniacal about his fitness.

"Better sign up for that nutrition class at the hospital," he said to Nora in between yet another set of pushups.

"I can't," Nora called from the kitchen. "We have to go to Cartersville that day to meet with the attorney. We won't be back in time."

"Damn it," Jimmy said, collapsing onto the floor. "I hate driving all that way. Why can't there be any decent lawyers here in Tillman?"

Nora carried a clothesbasket of freshly folded laundry to the bedroom and sidestepped past Jimmy, now doing a set of stomach crunches. He had rearranged their modest bedroom to accommodate some hand weights and workout space to use in addition to time he spent at the gym favored by firemen.

"It's really not that far," Nora said. She squeezed around the edge of the bed to put clothes into a nicked and shabby chest of drawers. "Besides, this will be the last time, maybe. Our attorney told me we might get a settlement offer now."

Jimmy stopped his exercise and sat on the floor, watching his wife. When she finished arranging clean clothes in their drawers, she turned to him and smiled. Reaching down, she smoothed a wrinkle from the bedspread and sat on the edge of the bed.

"Nora," Jimmy said. He hunched over looking at his feet. "What if we don't get a settlement? I mean, there is that chance, you know."

"We will–after everything you've been through." She stood with the empty clothesbasket, but sat back down when Jimmy raised his head.

"It's not about what I've been through. It's not even about how serious my injuries were or how long I was off work. It's about responsibility."

"But you saved so many people on that train." Nora's eyes were wide and guileless.

"And did I have to do it?" he asked. "Hell yes, I'd say. That's my job and more than that, my duty. But Nora, was it the railroad's fault?" Jimmy shook his head. "I wish I could say I think it was, but the truth is that woman in the minivan caused it."

"Poor thing," Nora said, looking down. "To die so young, with those little children too."

"Yeah, it's sad, but she wasn't poor, Nora." Jimmy's eyes glinted as he moved closer to her. "She was the wife of Ben Richards, the guy they accused me of shooting in that hunting accident. Me! The guy who risks his life every day to save people on the job."

He sat on the bed and took her hand in his. "They tried to incriminate me, Nora, and me being shot too. You remember how it was–newspaper articles, accusations, me having to go to depositions in pain and on crutches…"

Nora pulled her hand away from Jimmy's, pressed her fingertips to her temples and shut her eyes. "Yes, yes, I want to forget it."

"Well, I haven't forgotten," Jimmy said, standing. "And this time I won't be their victim. I'm the only one who knows what really happened at Cedar Woods."

4

Schemes

Leland Richards glided into the opulent boardroom of GillRich Construction Company. His well-groomed silver hair shone like sunlight glimmering through gleaming windows. A faint aura of cigar smoke entered the room with him. Every board member was in place around the polished oval table surrounded by windows on three sides; John's idea to promote openness and equality among board members, and Leland had conceded to it. *No more concessions.*

He boomed greetings in a hearty voice of practiced authority. Thomas Eikens and Marsh Dalton continued to lean toward each other, speaking in hushed tones. Leland dismissed the old guard, as he liked to call them, like-minded colleagues of his former partner, John Gilliver. It would be difficult for them to refute numbers and his chairmanship now.

"Gentlemen," he said, standing until each board member looked at him. "Let's begin, shall we?" He sat, erect and ebullient. He did not open the folder before him on the table.

"Today it is my very great pleasure to announce last quarter's earnings are the highest in the history of our company." Polite applause demonstrated the board's conservative nature and continued skepticism toward his leadership.

"As you know, the project honoring our former chairman and Tillman's former mayor, John Gilliver, was subject to much debate among us, but I am proud to say all contracts have been signed. Obstacles for land acquisition have been overcome. We expect no further legal challenges."

Thomas Eikens coughed presumptively. He began to speak without first requesting permission from the chair, annoying Leland. "Now I thought we had not come to a conclusion about that folly, Gilliver House Hotel. The cart is way before the horse on this one."

Leland pounded his fist on the stately table. "Damn it, Tom. We've been through all this, and I'll thank you to not interrupt me. The project has been voted on and the only two dissenting votes, as you well know, were from you and Marsh. You're done, over, finished."

Thomas Eikens stood. His grandfatherly appearance with his stooped posture, rumpled suit and balding, pug-nosed profile did not disguise the fire in his bespectacled eyes. "Gentlemen, it is a travesty that a hotel honoring John Gilliver, a man who stood for honesty and integrity, who built this company's reputation for fairness through providing a quality product and years of community service, who led us to—"

"Oh, for Christ's sake, Tom," Leland said. "It's a done deal. We're building the damn hotel the way I intend to build it and that's final. Furthermore, look at these figures on the chart inside your folder." Leland waved a colored graphic printed on expensive bond. "I put these numbers into triple digits in the profit column. Not John."

"And we all know how you did it, Leland," Marsh Dalton said in his whispery rasping voice. "Hiring scab labor, displacing our suppliers in favor of cheap foreign shipments of questionable quality, fudging on specifications. It's only a matter of time until we get lawsuits for shoddy construction on those last two projects. John would never have done that."

The other board members nodded until Leland exploded again. He resented the saintly reference to his former business partner, especially from that self-serving town banker. "Let's be real here. Marsh and Tom and any of the rest of you who think I'm not running this company in our best interests." Leland looked at faces around the table. "I know John was a good man, but in the last six years, we've made more money than we did in the previous twenty. And it's because of me. It's a different world out there, a different environment for doing business. Old ways are out the window. We have to compete in a global economy, even here in Tillman."

Without exception, the board members looked down, studying graphic representations of the company's financial picture in their opened folders. *Now I've got them. By God, I won't let those two old hacks get away with challenging me.*

Leland composed himself and smiled. Leaning forward, he said, "As you can see, we are now in a position to move ahead with negotiations for my next proposal."

Sylvia avoided Brian. She told Marianna she had a massive headache and needed to lie down, undisturbed, in her room. Usually Brian ignored messages from servants, but after the sound of both the arrival and departure of his sports car in the circular driveway, she opened French doors from her room onto a broad balcony and settled into a chaise lounge to watch gathering deep blue twilight creep over tree-tops. A gentle breeze smelling of honeysuckle lifted slight perspiration from her skin. It was a perfect summer night, except for the chilly lump within her.

Sylvia willed her thoughts to silence, watching wispy clouds dissipate with encroaching dusk. Below her the gazebo was in its summer glory surrounded by green with shiny leaves of perennial ivy winding around the railing on one side. This was the scene of so many happy family gatherings. Sad times too.

Gazing dreamily at the gazebo, she envisioned Lisa Gilliver wearing a lavender scarf over a jewel-necked white blouse with a perfectly tailored black suit, swingy dark straight hair, and large gray eyes, a family trait. She looked lawyerly, Sylvia mused. Lisa had graduated from the same law school as Brian, same year, only weeks before Daddy had died. She had been buoyed with the promise of future success.

Only Lisa had enough moxie to wear lavender to her father's funeral. Sylvia recalled her sister flirting, even on that somber occasion. When they gathered after the service, every man there clustered around her. Leland Richards, her father's business partner, had dominated the group, putting his arm around Lisa's shoulders and steering her away from her law school friends, including Brian, toward his athletic and handsome son, Ben. They had all known each other since childhood, of course, but something was different between Ben and Lisa that day.

Brian, dressed impeccably as usual, had comforted Sylvia in her sorrow, but his eyes followed Lisa's movements among the crowd.

She shut her eyes to the specter of a loveless marriage and convinced herself it would all work out in time, recalling a conversation with Lisa before her wedding.

"Isn't this just the best time of your life? So far, I mean," Sylvia had said during Lisa's final fitting for her wedding gown.

Lisa ignored the seamstress and stepped over to Sylvia, taking Sylvia's hands in her own and speaking with an earnest intensity. "Listen, little sister, not everything in life is as rosy as Mother led us to believe."

Sylvia was astonished. She gazed into Lisa's serious eyes, gray like storm clouds.

"This wedding is for her, what she would have wanted, and for Daddy. I'm marrying his closest business partner's son. Ben's father would not let our wedding be any less lavish because I'm an orphan."

"I'm an orphan too," Sylvia had said.

Today, a pang of nostalgia for a happy home life surprised her. *Was it a trick of memory or fantasy of an innocent youth?*

After returning from an extravagant Hawaii honeymoon, Brian put his arms around Sylvia, pulling her close. "I guess now we can file papers to change the deed," he said, brushing her hair with his lips.

"Change the deed?"

"Well sure, darling," he said. "Now that we're man and wife both our names should be on the property deed."

Sylvia laughed, masking her uneasiness. "Brian," she said, circling her index finger on his chest, "You are certainly in a hurry to get under the black cloud that hovers over this family. It's too soon. Now that I'm home all the deaths and the uncertainty about Grace weigh me down. I can't even think of it now."

"Okay, darling," Brian gave her a tight-lipped smile. "I didn't mean to upset you. If you're not ready yet, that's okay. But it's for Grace that I want to do it."

"What do you mean? Grace is gone, dead or, I don't know what. I only wish she could inherit."

"Of course, when she shows up, she'll be an heir."

Sylvia's gray eyes turned poisonous. *What does that have to do with putting his name on the deed?* "What about our children, Brian? I assume we'll have some." *Why didn't we talk about children?*

"In due time, but let's not talk about it anymore now. I'll get the paperwork together at the office and wait until you're ready to file it. Meanwhile, you can start redecorating."

"I have a job, remember?"

"Oh that's easy enough to give up. It's not a real job anyway."

"You're sure anxious to take control."

"Somebody has to," Brian said, "and I am your husband now, darling." He turned to check the time on the antique grandfather clock in the foyer. "Like, for example, that clock needs to be refitted. It's always ten minutes fast."

Sylvia started to explain her mother's trick to fool her dawdling little girls into being on time. But she didn't. The first brick in the wall between them had been laid. It startled her and also comforted her. *Marriage doesn't mean I need to surrender the home of my inheritance and memories of my life to him.*

Brian said, "Well, I'm off to check on a few things at the office. I won't be late." He kissed her forehead and sauntered away.

She thought of her sister again, and her remembered words floated into the room like a ghost. Sylvia shivered. *I always wanted to be more like you, Lisa. Now, I guess I am.*

Brian Boggs and Leland Richards met for a circumspect lunch nearly every month. Brian was all too willing to step into the shoes, and inheritance, of Leland's son, Ben. In fact, Brian harbored a secret he planned never to share with anyone. It gave him a sense of entitlement.

They always lunched at Tillman's private country club where Leland was a charter member. When Brian arrived first, he was shown to Leland's favorite table and his customary single malt scotch materialized within moments.

Brian took a drink and gazed out the window to as fine a natural view as the season in Tillman could offer. Leland clamped his left hand on Brian's shoulder and extended his right for a handshake. "Mr. Boggs," he said. "Nice to have lunch with my almost relative, my own private, private attorney." He winked at Brian as he slid into his chair and reached for the perfect dry martini at his place.

"Those company attorneys drive me mad, but you, my boy," Leland tasted his drink, "well, let's just say we have a special project together."

"Yes, indeed," Brian said in a low voice. "Something has happened since last month. It's slow going, but I've peeled away a layer of disguise from the trust documents." Brian paused.

Leland's eyes glinted. "Go on."

"Well, as I said, it's slow going because the properties are mired in tangles of legal tax and ownership protection. But we now know the listed ownership trust, for tax purposes, is legal fiction, a paper entity with no other reason for existence."

"I don't like the way you say we." Leland moved closer to Brian.

"A figure of speech," Brian said. They both leaned back to give their orders to a lingering waiter. Both always ordered their steaks rare and their potatoes baked with sour cream, but they suffered through the wait staff's recitation of specials. A second round of drinks appeared on the starched white tablecloth.

"Moreover," Brian said when the waiter was gone, "someone has taken precise legal maneuvers to stall the investigation there. The ownership of each of the houses and the entire parcel of land they comprise is well hidden. We're–I'm–onto something now for one of the pieces and it may turn out to be the same for the others."

"Well," Leland said, stroking his chin in a habitual manner. "I had a feeling there was a reason that area remained undeveloped. But I had no idea it was a hidden tax shelter."

"Mired in liens and numbered trust accounts like I've never seen. Disguised to thwart the ordinary real estate inquiry."

"But there's nothing ordinary about our little conspiracy, is there?" Leland asked.

"No." Brian replied as the silent waiter laid noiseless plates in front of each of them. *Nothing ordinary about me either.*

Leland Richards drummed his fingertips on the boardroom table. He listened with fierce intensity to his colleague, Thomas Eikens.

"I don't understand why we should ask our investors to participate in this folly on the west side." Thomas made eye contact around the table with a smile. "Gentlemen, there's nothing going on in that direction. The town's growth is eastward and then south along the river valley. Senator Greene has assured us, well practically speaking; the legislature is set to pass the bill containing a generous grant for development all along the river corridor in this part of the state. Tillman's leading developers," he smiled again, "stand to get a generous allowance for any project we undertake. We need to move on riverfront condominiums and mall plans. Once we get zoning approval, of course, which won't be difficult."

"Your turn to put the cart before the horse, eh, Tom?" Leland asked. "We don't even have the land yet." He smirked.

"True enough," Thomas said. "But that's where the appropriation is intended to be spent. Surely we can get our land acquisition attorneys to work on it. I'm telling you, somebody's going to buy that property for development and it might as well be us."

Marsh Dalton cleared his throat. "Tom," he said, "this is one area where I have to agree with Leland, though I admit it's unusual for me to do that." Polite chuckles rippled through the boardroom.

Standing, he gestured in the river's direction as he continued. "There's nothing but ratty old houses and a few provincial businesses in the area between the tracks and the river flood plain, excepting mostly deserted railroad yards. It's the least desirable part of Tillman. Nobody's going to want to live there."

"That's what development means," Thomas said. "My proposal includes commercial projects that would draw tenants and business owners. Condominiums would be a natural outgrowth of revitalized economy in that section of town. The government is willing, so we are led to believe, to fund infrastructure that would be needed and also lean on the railroad to abandon those run down yards for a more advantageous location to the north. We stand to get in on the ground floor of a major improvement that will draw investors from this whole part of the state."

Murmurs of approval accompanied nodding agreement. Marsh was seated again with his arms crossed, frowning.

"Well, you're all a bunch of fools," Leland said. "All the money in Tillman is on the west side, above the bluffs. And, I'm happy to say the Gilliver House Hotel is soon to break ground. We can still get government money for projects surrounding it, for Christ's sake. The risk to our investors is far less and the potential for profits is far greater. I don't intend to put any of my support into this east side folly–your term, Thomas."

"I propose a motion to table this discussion of an east side development." Marsh Dalton rasped with authority. "We need to do some research before jumping into what I still think is a bad idea."

"I second," Leland said. "Now, all in favor?"

A chorus of grudging and reluctant 'ayes' resounded. Thomas shook his head and said "Nay," loud and clear.

Leland smiled with satisfaction and deftly moved the meeting onto the next item on the agenda.

Footsteps echoed on the sidewalk behind Thomas Eikens after he left his favorite restaurant in a fashionable area of Tillman. Clouds obscured the moon and a cooling summer thunderstorm was building overhead. Thomas was lost in thought as he made his way a few blocks toward his parked car.

The pace of footsteps quickened. When Thomas passed a darkened storefront his right arm was wrenched and twisted behind him while a gloved hand reached around his head to cover his mouth. He struggled but his left leg was kicked out from under him and he stumbled.

Roughly, he was shoved into the vestibule of the closed shop. Overcome by the smell of beer breath on his assailant, he gagged. Panic washed over him. His face was slammed into a shadowy corner and he gasped for breath. *What the hell?*

"I got a message for you, Gramps," said the voice attached to the stinking breath close to his ear. "Forget your plans for the east side. Drop it or die."

The man yanked on his contorted arm. Thomas cried out in pain but the gloved hand pressing on his face muffled the sound. His attacker pushed him to the ground as a flash of lightning illuminated the man's face. "Who are you?" Thomas yelled.

But he ran into darkness leaving Thomas with only the diminishing sounds of his footsteps. Fat raindrops fell with fury.

5

Secrecy

Mae trudged the icy sidewalk to the hospital employee's entrance. So far, so good. For over six months she had more than tasted the joy of motherhood; she'd embraced it. She'd reveled in it. Now, tonight, an important piece she needed to make Amy permanently hers would fall into place. Her heart fluttered.

Inside the antiseptic smelling nurse's workstation on the pediatric ward, Mae took pleasure in the simple order that had always comforted her there. She looked over the patient's charts and made notations. She clamped her emotions as idle chatter flew between nurses and aides changing shifts.

"You sure look happy tonight," Crystal Winston, a coworker on the shift said.

"Just about as happy as I can be," Mae said, pretending interest in the chart before her.

"Well, praise the Lord for that," Crystal said. "Motherhood agrees with you. How much longer will you be taking care of that sweet little angel of your sister's?"

"Indefinitely. Pat doesn't seem to be getting any better right now," Mae said, frowning. "But it's okay. I love her like my own."

"I don't remember you talking about your family. How many sisters do you have?"

"Only the one." Mae stomach knotted. *One more lie.*

Crystal looked at her for a moment then said, "I'd better go look in on the Sanders' family. It's such a shame what they're going through with their baby." Crystal shook her head.

Mae nodded agreement. "Awful," she said. But as Crystal walked toward the pediatric intensive care waiting room, Mae suppressed a smile. She had been waiting and watching for this night. Mike and Donna Sanders' baby would likely die tonight. She felt sorry for them and for their tiny, emaciated child. But little Lillian Sanders would be the first baby matching Amy's blood type, race and approximate date of birth to die in their hospital since Mae had conceived her idea. She knew she had to establish Amy's identification separately, and Mae had access to hospital records.

Moreover, their baby had been born in another county, not far from where Mae pretended her sister lived. Donna Sanders had delivered prematurely while visiting family. Mae pitied Donna, whose baby had been in the hospital more often than not since her birth. Then, Mike Sanders had been seriously injured in the train accident that had brought Amy to Charlie and Mae.

At least something good came of it. Mae rifled through the extensive file selecting birth certificate and immunization records to be copied, altered and reproduced with Amy's name. This was so much easier than finding an obituary of an infant's death and going to the courthouse for its birth certificate. *I'm doing this for you, Charlie, honey. Amy belongs with us. We'll be the best parents in the world for that little girl.*

Mae shivered then at the thought of Charlie's flecked brown eyes. Honest even if against his own interest. He might be made to lie; she was sure of that, but not with those eyes. She would have to watch him closely.

Charlie cooed to baby Amy as he fed her strained carrots. She smiled between mouthfuls, and three new teeth glinted among orange goop.

"Soon as you eat, little one," Charlie said, "we'll get you all clean to go see your mommy at work, okay?"

At hearing the word mommy, Amy clapped her hands together, grinning. She smashed carrot drops on her highchair tray while bouncing and flailing her arms, mouth open for more. Orange specks splattered Charlie's shirt.

"Oh my," Charlie said with mock dismay. "Now I have to change my shirt too." He winked at Amy as he scooped another spoonful into her mouth. "I'll tell you a little secret," he whispered, leaning closer to the baby whose big eyes got wider. "Daddy's going to work this afternoon."

Storm clouds blew into Amy's gray eyes where only sunshine had been.

"Only for a little while." Charlie dipped the tiny spoon into the carrots again.

As if she understood, Amy's sunny mood returned as quickly as it had gone, and she clamped onto the spoon, pumping her arms and spraying him with strained carrots again.

Charlie hurried along the hospital sidewalk amid cold snow flurries toward the employee's entrance carrying a well-wrapped sleeping baby and a diaper bag. Mae met him just inside.

"I'll be done when you get home, I think," he said, passing Amy to the waiting arms.

"Call me and I'll come get you." Mae rose on her toes to kiss him on the cheek.

"She's been fed and bathed. Plus there's an extra change of clean clothes."

Mae loosened the blanket around the sleeping child. "You always take such good care of her, Charlie. I'm so lucky, I mean, we're so lucky." In her strong arms she shifted Amy's weight and smiled down, rearranging the chubby cheek and rosebud lips resting against her chest.

Mae worked the day shift now, for a time, to replace another nurse who was on maternity leave. It was an easy matter for her to keep Amy at work on the pediatric ward when Charlie got these short referral jobs, working for cash.

When she turned to walk back to her work area, cradling Amy, Mae blew a kiss to Charlie. He watched them for a few moments before he hurried along the blustery sidewalk, now filmed with light snow. *Yes, I'm lucky too. Very lucky.*

Charlie's days and nights revolved around Amy: Caring for her, watching her sleep and most fun of all, playing with her. He rolled the soft plastic ball to her for hours, delighting in her delight.

She loved to sit on the kitchen vinyl floor, chipped but clean, and bang on pots and pans with wooden spoons and measuring cups. Always, he kept her close, and when she was awake, he often talked to her.

"Some guys who get jobs for me might think I'm crazy, or bored," he said to Amy. She slobbered and grinned, showing off two new teeth.

"But I'm happier than any of them." He tousled Amy's fine dark hair as he sidestepped her mixing bowls to put away clean dishes. He squatted to watch her intent expression as she tried to put a one cup plastic measure into a half cup one.

"See, Amy, I've got Mae and she loves me. And now we've got you to love together."

Amy thrust the measuring cups away from her with one determined movement and lifted her sturdy baby arms to Charlie, drooling. He scooped her up and stood in one quick motion, reaching for a fresh towel to wipe her face. He kept talking as he held her in one arm and walked around the kitchen putting things in order.

"I take good care of my girls," he said. "That makes me happy. Those guys don't know what they're missing."

Charlie settled Amy into the highchair and poured some cheerios onto the tray. Amy grasped some in her chubby palm and stuck them into her mouth, eyes shining. Charlie poured a cup of coffee and sat next to her at the table.

"So, Mae says she has it all worked out, with papers and all, so we can keep you forever."

Amy grunted.

"Or, at least until you grow up," he said. "See, we found you, after the train wreck, but that's our little secret." He held his finger to his lips for silence. Amy mimicked him clumsily.

"Never, never, Mae says, should we ever tell anybody. And she's smart, little girl. We have to believe her." A sudden cloud darkened the new spring sunshine outside, and Charlie felt a chill in his heart. He shook off the feeling. *Whoever lost you couldn't love you as much as we do.*

Amy pounded the highchair tray with grubby fists, and Charlie reached for more Cheerios.

Donna and Mike Sanders buried their beautiful Lillian and mourned for several weeks. Their grief simmered, then turned black, evil and strong.

"You would think that damn lawyer would have something for us by now," Mike said one morning. He kicked the rickety kitchen table making their coffee cups rattle and jump. "When did he say he'd get back to you?"

"He didn't. He said he'd be in touch, and we've been so preoccupied." Donna brushed a tear away. "But there's something strange about that guy, Mike," she said. "I knew I'd seen him somewhere, but my mind's been in such a fog. I can almost remember."

"Well, strange or not, he'd better return our call this time." Mike set his jaw in determined defiance. "Or else. I still can't go back to work, and I'm not even sure those idiots at the fire station will take me back. But there are other things I can do." His eyes flickered toward the kitchen cabinet where he kept his guns. "I don't want you out there cleaning those rich folks' houses anymore either."

"Mike," Donna said, pleading. "It's only until you get back to work or we get a settlement. We need to pay bills."

"Hell, it doesn't even do that." Mike punched one fist into his other palm. "That stupid loan company keeps calling about truck payments. I told them it took everything we had for Lillian. Can't they see the railroad owes me something? Or the city?"

Donna put a hand on her husband's arm. "Why don't you go see Mr. Boggs, honey?" she said. "Maybe he'll get the message that we need money better from you than from me."

"Yeah," he said. "Who does he think we are? No wife of mine should have to clean their dirty stuff–"

"That's it!" Donna's face brightened and she jumped to her feet. "That's where I've seen him. I knew it!"

"What are you talking about?" Mike's irritability grew.

"That attorney, Brian Boggs. I saw him at Gilliver's river cabin when I went there to clean one time. It was a long time ago, before, before Lillian was born." A shadow crossed her features. "But I remember now," she said. "He was with that woman who got killed in the train crash. And, they were mighty cozy. In fact, I walked in when he was pulling up his pants."

Now Mike's demeanor brightened too. "Are you saying he was with a married woman?"

Donna looked into the distance. "It had to be before her husband got shot in that hunting accident because they closed the river cabin for a while after that. When Marianna called me again, I said I couldn't clean it because I was pregnant with Lillian."

Mike had turned a shade paler at hearing her mention the hunting accident, but he quickly recovered. "You mean…?"

"Yes, I think he was with her before she lost her husband. I wonder if his wife knows."

"Oh, this is juicy." Mike rubbed his hands together. "Maybe I will go pay him a visit. And, you'd better go back to cleaning that cabin, for a bit," he said. He stroked her arm in a loving gesture but his eyes glinted. "Who knows what else you might find out?"

A staff of paralegals and secretaries scurried around the law offices of Brian Boggs. The boss was on a rampage. When the front door flew open with a bang, they froze.

"I want to see that son-of-a-bitch," Mike Sanders said. No one made a move to stop him from barging into Brian's private office.

"What kind of a lawyer are you?" Mike bellowed as he strode to Brian's desk and stood there glaring at him with his hands on his hips. The smell of stale beer came in with him.

"Hold on," Brian said, lifting his palms up in front of him. With his foot hidden under the desk, he switched on his secret tape recorder.

"My wife has been calling you and all she gets is your damn secretary saying she'll take a message. Does this mean you're not getting us any money?"

"No."

"No!" Mike's face filled with rage.

"I mean, not yet. Not yet, man. These things take time. Now, Mr. Sanders, is it? Why don't you have a seat and we'll discuss your case?" Brian said.

"I'm tired of talk. All you lawyers are good at is talk and double talk. That's what I say."

Mike kicked the chair and pushed it close to the front of Brian's desk before he sat down.

"Mr. Sanders, let me assure you—"

"Don't assure me anything. You know what we've been through, with our little Lillian and all. And I can't work, except for these…"

"These?" asked Brian.

Mike stared at him. "That's none of your business. A man has to do what a man has to do. You just get me the money."

"Um, yes, well, the worker's compensation benefits must have provided some relief."

"Ha! That chicken feed. Plus they're telling me the firemen's fund has no more money for me and they're not hiring me back. This after I saved all those people before I got hurt."

"Mr. Sanders—"

Mike narrowed his eyes. "Look, I was in the hospital for a long time. I had plenty of time to think and the way I see it, the railroad owes me. Big time. Now, are you going to do something about it?"

"We filed your lawsuit, Mr. Sanders, well within the statute of limitations and it's moving through the court system. But surely you must realize many cases have arisen from that accident, and there are several parties for the railroad to address."

"I don't give a crap about all those others. You need to get in their face and get our case settled. Or else."

"Are you threatening me, Mr. Sanders? Because if you are—"

"Because what? I'll tell you. There might be somebody who saw something you did. Something with that rich lady at her river house."

Brian blanched. Mike smirked, pushed back his chair and stood. "See, I thought so," he said. "But don't worry. Your dirty little secret is safe with me, for now. I'm giving you one more week to come up with some money."

"That's impossible! You don't understand the complexity of these negotiations."

"Well, maybe not." Mike smiled for the first time in their meeting. "But I do understand one more week, Mr. Lawyer-man."

With that, Mike Sanders turned and stomped out of the law office, slamming the door behind him.

6

Awareness

Charlie sometimes sat on the front stoop facing Sparrow Street after Mae went to work to relive events that had brought Amy to them. The years were passing in a contented glow as he repaired and restored the sagging house.

Amy grimaced in concentration over letters on the paper in front of her. Then, cheering up, she said, "I know, Daddy." She jumped in her excitement then plopped down onto the step. She grabbed the pencil in a determined fist and pressed out the letters **d o g.**

What if I hadn't picked her up? She would have died. Charlie shuddered.

"I did it! I did it! Look, Daddy, look." Amy held out the paper to Charlie. She danced from one foot to another.

What if I had taken her to the police? Or the hospital?

"That's wonderful, Amy." He studied the page. "Tell you what. Let's play catch now. You've been working so hard on your letters."

"No, Daddy, I love to write." Her face was a jubilant glow in the sunshine. She snatched the paper from his hand and ran into the house.

Charlie turned away and blinked back tears. *It's not always easy to know the right thing to do.* A breeze rattled shutters on the front window. Charlie shook off a chill and got up. *Guess now I'll have to take the consequences, right or wrong.* The wind gusted and shook the shutters again as he went inside.

Amy thrived. In school she was bright, chatty and thoroughly well-behaved. Other children liked her and soon invitations for play-dates came.

"Daddy, please," Amy said. "Please can I go to Sarah's on Saturday?"

"I'll think about it," Charlie said. "I told you, we have to talk to Mommy first."

Amy galloped around the room chanting, "Mommy say yes! Mommy say yes!"

When Mae came home from work, Amy pounced on her. "Mommy, Sarah says I can go over to her house to play. Can I? Can I go, Mommy?"

Mae stooped to Amy's eye level. "That's really nice, Amy. I'll think about it. Let me talk to your Daddy first."

Amy stomped her feet and crossed her arms. "You and Daddy said the same thing! Why can't I go? Why?" She pouted. Tears filled her eyes.

"Because, honey," Mae dumped her purse and car keys onto the battered kitchen table. "If you go to Sarah's to play, we should invite her to play here too. Sometime."

Amy brightened. "That's okay. Sarah can come here too." She reached for Mae's hand and stood on tiptoe to whisper, "You know, we have lots of playing to do."

In an abrupt movement, she let go of Mae's hand and skipped into the living room, then up bare wooden steps to her bedroom. "Daddy, Daddy, where are you? Mommy says Sarah can come here to play too."

"Oh she does, does she?" Charlie stopped folding Amy's clean clothes to pick her up and swing her around. She squealed in delight. Setting her down, he took her hand. "Well, let's go talk to Mommy right now."

Amy scrambled downstairs to the kitchen where Mae sat, work shoes off, rubbing her feet. "Mommy, Daddy says we are going to talk to you RIGHT NOW."

Charlie appeared in the doorway. "How was your day, honey?" He gave Mae a kiss and hug.

"Busy," Mae said. "There are so many kids admitted with respiratory infections lately." She smiled at Amy who was now dressing a doll and humming. "Thank God she hasn't caught anything. Yet."

"Amy," Charlie said, "let's show Mommy what you learned to do after school today."

Amy dropped the doll and bounded toward Mae with her lips pursed. She made a faint and breathy sound. "See, I did it, Mommy. Daddy taught me. I whistle." She continued to puff faint notes as she marched around the house, stopping only to talk to her Dolly. "Sarah's going to like you."

Mae sighed and looked at Charlie. He shrugged. "What can it hurt?"

Mae replied in a low voice. "I think you know perfectly well." They both turned to look at Amy, now preoccupied with emptying the contents of her small toy box onto the living room floor.

"We can't keep her home with me forever," Charlie said. "Now that she's in school—"

"I know." Mae rested her chin on her hand. "She will want to spend more and more time with her little friends. I wish we could keep her with us like this forever."

"But I don't want her to be like me. She's smart, Mae, like you." Charlie caressed his wife's neck, and she relaxed at his touch.

"I'm afraid, though, Charlie," Mae whispered. "Maybe we should move away. Far enough so no one will know. Or remember."

She shivered in spite of the warm autumn day. He stopped rubbing her neck and came around to sit in front of her, taking her hands in his. "I'll do whatever you want, Mae. But this house is ours, thanks to Nana, and you have a job. I only get side jobs as a carpenter. How can we afford to move?"

Unopened mail on the clean but stained counter top. A stack of bills again. Her kitchen had chipped Formica, cracked plastic wall tile and worn vinyl flooring, but also well-tended, nourished houseplants on the windowsill, sun shining through immaculate windows and simmering stew on the stove. Loving care was everywhere, especially in Charlie's concerned brown eyes.

"Oh Charlie," she said. "We are so happy here–with Amy."

"So we are okay then? We'll get by, honey."

Mae braved a smile into her husband's tender eyes and pushed all doubt and fear from her mind.

Charlie walked the floors at night, slipping out of bed like a snake not to wake Mae. Often, he paused to watch exceptional peace on her sleeping face before creeping to Amy's room. There he pulled up the covers she usually kicked off in the night and watched her for a few moments.

Downstairs, he went outside, in all kinds of weather except rain because he didn't want Mae to smell his wet skin when he slid back into bed. If it was cloudless, he wanted to check the night's constellations. His grandmother taught them all by name and in the night she was close to him again. For some reason, he'd never shared his love of the night stars with either Mae or Amy. It was as if he kept them to himself with his memories of his Nana. It also gave him time to think.

Amy was having fun in school, he hoped. He wanted her to have the chance to feel special. Unlike him. Well, he had felt special too, like walking with rocks in his shoes.

Charlie had started out full of energy, like any other six year old. But it soon became clear he didn't see things the same way as the other children. He learned differently in a classroom setting that didn't allow for it. His first grade teacher had ridiculed him, and he came home crying.

His grandmother, Lorraine, knelt to hug and hold him. "What's wrong? What happened at school? Now you tell me, Charlie."

When he told her what the teacher had said, she'd immediately straightened. "That is absolutely NOT true." She reached for her purse and held out her hand to Charlie. "We're going to go back there right now and talk to her."

"Oh no," Charlie had cried. "I don't want to go back there, ever, please Nana."

His grandmother's eyes flashed, but she said only, "This time you'll be with me, Charlie. Don't be afraid. Don't ever be afraid."

Following her, Charlie could barely move his legs, wooden and slow. The teacher was surprised when Lorraine burst into her classroom. "I'm sorry," she said. "I'm getting ready to leave. Did you have an appointment?" Then she saw Charlie, red-faced, peeking out from behind his Nana's skirt, and she said, "Oh."

"Oh?" Lorraine strode across the classroom. "I'll bet you know why I'm here."

The teacher's upper lip curled as she took in Lorraine's shabby dress and worn shoes. "I can assure you, I don't, Mrs. ... Jericho? Is it?"

"You can get off your high horse right now," Lorraine said. "You know damn good and well who I am and who this child is, my grandson. Don't pretend otherwise, or is lying all you know how to do?"

"Certainly not." The teacher stood and drew herself to her full height, still a bit shorter than Lorraine.

"How dare you tell my grandson he's learning disabled? Don't you know the difference from learning differently? And worthless? You ought to be ashamed."

The teacher took a step backwards, stumbling over her chair. "Well, he simply is, that's all. I'm the teacher and I know how far behind the other children he is. He shouldn't even be in this school, or at least not in my class."

Lightning fast, Lorraine slapped her. The teacher screamed and struck out but wasn't fast enough. Lorraine grabbed a fistful of the teacher's hair and said, "You listen to me. If ever I hear of you talking to this child like that again, you'll regret it. And I mean it." The teacher pushed back and began to cry. "You should give every child a chance to feel special. How do you expect them to learn?"

A big man came running into the room and pushed himself in between the two women. There was shouting and Charlie heard words like retarded and threatened. The next thing he knew, his Nana wheeled around and took his hand as she marched out of the school.

"What happened, Nana?" Charlie was even more afraid of his teacher now. He sobbed.

Lorraine stopped then, bent to look him in the eye. "Don't worry, child. I'm never taking you back to that school again."

So, Charlie reasoned as he had so many times, that's why he couldn't read and hadn't gone to school. It was his fault. If he hadn't told Nana about what the teacher said, well, no sense thinking about that now. His grandmother kept him at home to teach him herself, which she had until she got sick. He'd learned his numbers and all the constellations of the night sky and how to take care of both of them.

Sylvia fidgeted in the clinic's waiting room. She faced the examination with a mixture of hope and dread. *Over five years now. I want to be pregnant, or at least I think I do. Brian says he wants it. His heir.*

While she paged through a *Good Housekeeping* magazine without really reading it, a forty-something couple came in with a young girl. They settled in the chairs across from Sylvia with the girl sitting between them.

"Now Amy," the woman said. "Today is a big day. You'll get your final immunizations for school."

"Will I have to get a shot?" Amy looked worried.

The man reached to pat her hand. "Well if you do, honey," he said, "it will all be for the good."

Sylvia studied them over the top of her opened magazine. Something about the way the little girl held her head reminded her of her sister, Lisa. She even had Lisa's shiny, straight dark hair. When the child looked toward her, Sylvia nearly gasped. She was looking into the image of her own large gray eyes.

"Isn't that a pretty lady, Mommy?" Amy asked, pointing toward Sylvia.

"Hush now, Amy," Mae said. "It's not polite to point at people."

Sylvia put down her magazine and openly stared at them. The man shifted in his chair and took the girl's hand in his. "Let's go look at toys the doctor has," he said, standing.

"Oh goody," Amy said. She bounded up and over to the corner with brightly colored blocks and plastic animals kept to occupy waiting children.

Sylvia's eyes followed their every movement. There was something familiar about the bearded man, who got down onto his knees to play with toys along with his daughter. As he put scattered pieces of an orange and yellow train together for her, he began to softly whistle.

Recognition shocked her. *That's where I've seen him. At the store by the railroad tracks after Lisa died. That girl, that little girl, looks just like my sister.*

She shifted her eyes toward the woman who had a strange expression on her face. I'm going to talk to her. But as she rose to cross the room, someone tapped her shoulder.

"I called your name twice, Mrs. Boggs," the nurse said, "but I guess you didn't hear me. The doctor is ready to see you now."

In slow motion, Sylvia followed the nurse. She had been openly staring at the girl. *She's about the right age.* When she came back into the waiting room, the family was gone.

"Where did that couple go, with the cute little girl?" she asked the receptionist.

"They had to leave," she said, a quizzical expression on her face.

"Well, who are they? I mean, what's their name? Where do they live?"

The receptionist spoke slowly, as if to a child. "Now, ma'am, you know I can't give you that information."

"I don't see why not." Sylvia turned on her heel and stomped off. *I'll think of a way to find out.*

"Hello, darling. How did it go?" Brian called when he came home. He crossed the living room to give Sylvia a kiss on the cheek as she sat looking out upon the autumn river scene.

"Huh? Oh, hi, what do you mean?" she asked, shaking herself out of her somber thoughts.

"Well the clinic, of course."

"No," Sylvia whispered. "No baby yet."

The smile on Brian's face faded. He went to the liquor cabinet to pour a scotch and returned to sit across from her. "I know you don't want to," he said, "but I think it's time for you to see that specialist we talked about."

"Me?" Sylvia asked. "Why not you? Why not both of us?"

"Because." Brian swirled ice chips in his drink. "Trust me on this, Sylvia. I know it's not me."

"What a lousy thing to say, Brian. You haven't had any children either."

Brian remained silent for a few moments. Then with a well-practiced, wistful expression he said, "But I want them. With you. It's up to you, Sylvia." He frowned. "I don't see why you don't want them as much as I do."

Sylvia sighed. *This same old argument.*

"I have something to tell you," she said. "Brian, I think I saw Grace today."

"What! How?" Brian's jaw dropped.

"At the clinic. A couple was there with a little girl about the same age as Grace would have been. She looked exactly like Lisa. Even to her facial expressions."

"Who are they?"

"I don't know but I'm going to find out."

As Brian made another drink, his face was deathly pale.

"I'll bring over the raffle tickets this afternoon for the benefit," Sylvia said into the phone. "That is, if you'll be home."

"Yes," said Janice Folger. "My daughter has invited a friend to play so I'll be here all day."

"See you then." Sylvia hung up.

"Who was that?" Brian asked.

He was jumpy about everything lately. Jumpy and suspicious.

"A woman from the hospital auxiliary, Brian. I'm delivering raffle tickets for the fall benefit this afternoon."

"Oh," Brian said. "Don't you think you're doing too much volunteer work? You've been working on this benefit for weeks now. And you still have that thing at the museum."

"Don't be silly," she said. "The Gilliver family has been involved in this charity for decades."

"Whatever you think." Brian shrugged. He sat down and shook open his newspaper.

Janice Folger answered on the first ring of the doorbell. She gave Sylvia a warm smile.

"Come in," she said. "Would you like a cup of coffee? Or perhaps some iced tea?"

"No thanks. I'll only need to count out tickets. How many did you say you wanted?"

"Sixty or seventy, I think," Janice replied. "Come into the kitchen and I'll help you count them."

Sylvia followed Janice through a short hallway that passed the family room doorway. "Thanks for helping with these," she said. "It's going to be another…"

She stopped walking after a glance into the family room, stifling a gasp. "Is that your daughter?"

"Yes." Janice turned back to stand with her, smiling. "My Sarah is the little blond and the dark-haired girl is her friend from school."

"Cute," said Sylvia, intentionally calm. "What's her friend's name?"

"Why, that's Amy. Amy Jericho."

At the sound of her name, Amy lifted her face with those huge gray eyes and the facial features that were so familiar to Sylvia.

"She looks like her mother."

"Well, no, not at all." Janice was puzzled. "Her mother is Mae Jericho from the hospital. She must favor her father." She resumed her way to the kitchen.

Sylvia followed her and counted out tickets with shaking hands.

"Is there something wrong?" Janice asked. "You look as if you've seen a ghost."

Maybe I have.

Brian sat with his elbows on his desk staring at a crumpled piece of paper smoothed out in front of him. *Must be from that crackpot Sanders.* He rubbed his temples and focused on the letters cut from magazines and glued individually onto the page.

TIME IS RUNING OUT

He can't even spell. Brian assessed his options. The railroad did seem close to settlement but could he count on them to close within a week? Less than that now. Or, should he consider other means?

He went to the well-stocked liquor cabinet in his office, but it was only 10:00 a.m. He turned away. *A bit too early, even for me. It wouldn't do to have Tillman's premier attorney drinking before noon, now would it?* He laughed out loud.

The telephone buzzed and his secretary's voice announced a call from his wife. He answered immediately.

"Brian, I'm going to hire a private investigator."

"Don't be rash, Sylvia. People will think you're crazy if it gets out."

"I don't care. I saw her, Brian. If you'd have seen her, you'd know she's Grace."

"Be reasonable. That accident was six years ago. Don't you think some evidence would have turned up by now?"

"No. Obviously. Seeing her was like looking at Lisa all over again. I have to know."

"So what do you plan to do?" Brian's palms were beginning to sweat. "Barge in and take that child away from her parents?"

"No, I plan to request a DNA test."

Now Brian jolted with panic. *Calm down. Calm down.* "Why would they allow you to do that?"

"That's where you come in, darling. There must be some kind of legal pretense you can dream up. You're good at that."

"Sylvia, do you know how swamped I've been lately?" Brian said in a chilly tone.

"Does that mean you're not going to help me?"

Brian took a deep breath. "Of course not, darling. But if you decide to go ahead with this, which I think is crazy-"

"I've decided."

"Well then." Brian gulped. "You better not do anything until you get the investigator's report."

They hung up and Brian considered it wasn't too early for that drink after all.

Immediately, another buzzing. His secretary told him Leland Richards was on the phone. Brian contemplated the threat letter on his desk and said, "Tell him I'm out."

7

Coincidence

"What really happened at Cedar Woods?" Nora asked.

Jimmy squinted at Nora. "I'm not sure I want you to know," he said. "It's for your own protection."

"I remember how frightened I was when they told me you'd been shot. You were in the hospital for the whole season. The awful police investigation and the lawsuit were almost worse. It's all a blur."

"It was a nightmare," Jimmy said. "I'm bitter, and I still can't get over how they accused me of killing Ben Richards when he's the one who shot me. He didn't mean to; I know that."

"How do you know? We've never talked about it."

"And we never will. It was so long ago, Nora," Jimmy's face had a pained expression. *Do I owe it to Nora to tell her? Considering what she's been through?*

"It's okay." Nora stroked his arm. "I'm relieved you're here with me now."

"As long as you understand, I'm grateful." Jimmy kissed her. "So, let's drop it, okay? I want to workout at the gym before my shift starts."

Jimmy wished he could forget. Once revived, the memory persisted no matter how long he ran on the treadmill. Usually his fanatical work-outs exorcised that particular demon, but not today. Jimmy was hitting his stride almost as soon as he jumped on the treadmill. He allowed himself to relive that day in Cedar Woods.

It was the dark, early morning of the First Annual Firemen's Benefit Deer Hunt. *The last too, as it turned out.* He envisioned the details.

That morning had given way to a beautiful fall day, crisp and cool. The foliage had begun to turn, but woodlands were still choked with summer growth, laden with a pungent edge. Rich local business-men had sponsored the event and offered the use of shotguns to those firemen who wanted to participate, free of charge. There were to be prizes and a fall cookout afterwards. Jimmy didn't have a decent gun, so he'd been happy to borrow one. *If only I'd known.*

They'd been organized into groups to ride into different sections of the woods for the hunt. Jimmy somehow ended up in a group with two sponsors, a banker named Marsh Dalton and the CEO of a very large construction company, Leland Richards and his son, Ben. They were all jovial, eager for the hunt and a great meal later at the cook-out. A part-time fireman named Mike Sanders had joined them at the last minute.

Jimmy remembered Mike was dressed in a heavy black sweat-shirt, black jeans and crepe-soled black shoes. It struck him as odd at the time. Everyone else had boots, and the others were dressed in their designer hunting gear. Jimmy had worn a hunting cap and jacket with jeans and boots.

Droplets of sweat flew off Jimmy as he pounded the tread, and his memories came alive.

"These guns are beauties," Mike had said to Jimmy. "Mossberg's."

Jimmy had shrugged. "Guess so. I really don't know much about them. Looks like they'll do the job."

"Yeah, the job," Mike had said, grinning.

"Now boys," Leland said when he drove their truck to the woods. "There's an old abandoned farm house bordering the far eastern edge of Cedar Woods. That property has been in my family for about 100 years, so I have rights to drive deer through its grounds. There's good cover–so much overgrowth where the deer love to hide. Lots of thorns though–multiflora roses, blackberry bushes, thick greenbrier vines."

"We've tracked here before," Marsh said. "Great cover. We'll drop you boys off at the end of a brushy fencerow so you can be standers. One of you will walk east about 80 to 100 yards and you'll see the other end of the old fencerow that goes along the eastern side of the abandoned farm orchards."

"I'll go," Ben said. "I've been there, and I'll show them."

"Now I think we only need two standers," Marsh said. "Jimmy, why don't you come with Leland and me? We go about a half mile back into the woods to drive deer toward the standers."

So it was decided. Jimmy was fully immersed in his memory as he mechanically adjusted the speed and slowed to a jog on the treadmill.

They had spread out in the dense foliage about 80 yards apart. It was like there was a curtain of green between them, redolent with the musky, moldy smell of thickly layered leaves and underbrush. Leland was far to the east, Marsh coming up the center and Jimmy to the west of him. No one spoke and each man was careful to maintain his distance, neither too far nor too close to each other. The drivers moved slowly, sometimes pausing to sit on tree stumps to listen and look for movement, but not to shoot unless the shot was clear or they were past the standers.

Marsh got a shot off and shouted, "It's mine!"

Jimmy's heart drummed, and he released the safety on his gun. Ben Richards moved out to his left and disappeared behind dense leaves only moments before an ear-stabbing shot and a shout was followed by still another booming discharge. In an instant a searing pain in his right side knocked him backwards causing him to drop his shotgun. He recalled the loud blast as his own gun went off close to his head.

Then he was falling, gasping for breath. His head twisted awkwardly. He saw Mike Sanders standing behind him, maybe twenty yards.

On the ground he struggled to stay conscious, pressing his now bloody hands onto the agony in his side. Marsh Dalton came running up to him shouting, "What have you done? What have you done?" Then Marsh was gone, and he heard a scream.

Leland Richards ran up to him then, white-faced, saying, "Oh no. Oh my god." Leland fumbled in several pockets of his hunting gear, shouting, "Marsh! There's a man down!" He found the cell phone, punched in some number and yelled their coordinates.

Marsh shouted, "Leland! Leland!" Then Mike Sanders ran up behind Leland. *How did he get there?* Jimmy tried to talk to Leland, saying, "He was behind me." But he was shivering and his teeth chattered.

Leland knelt beside him. "Don't worry son. Help is coming. Don't try to talk now." He had taken off his jacket and put it over Jimmy's chest.

Marsh was still calling Leland. Mike went crashing toward the sound of Marsh's voice as blackness rolled across Jimmy's vision.

I didn't know Mike Sanders. Only that he was around the firehouse sometimes. I didn't really know any of them until that day. Jimmy collapsed against the treadmill's console, turning it off. Panting and with a shaky hand, he draped a towel over his hanging head to absorb the sweat and to hide his tears.

The after-effects of the storm were in Sylvia's bones. She hurried down the broad museum steps to her ancient Saab, praying it would turn over. Sometimes in the wetness after a soaking downpour, Iris, the name she privately gave to her car, wouldn't start.

Brian cringed when she drove it. He made sure she had a new Lexus, which she did like and drive, but she couldn't part with Iris, her first car and the one her father had given her on her sixteenth birthday.

The starter ground two times. "Come on," she said aloud. On the third try, the engine sputtered to life, and Sylvia pressed ever so smoothly with a practiced, timid pressure on the gas pedal. "Good girl, Iris," she said, patting the dashboard with an automatic fondness. After a quick look into her rear view mirror, she pulled out into traffic.

The urgent patter of large drops mixing with the delayed creak of windshield wipers kept her on edge as she sped past Brian's office building, not wanting to be seen. He didn't approve of her position as Assistant Curator at the Tillman Art and History Museum but was careful to save his scorn for things like Iris instead of Sylvia's love of art. The Gilliver family tended toward practical but powerful occupations, such as Medicine or the Law. Her complete lack of interest in practical matters had confounded and frustrated her father. She sighed. *Well, no matter. I am happy with what I do even if it doesn't pay well or give me enormous prestige. I don't need the money anyway. Thank you very much, Daddy.*

At a seedy building next to a truck stop at the end of the city limits, she pulled her car to an abrupt stop. The diesel fumes from the array of parked semis nearly choked her when she hopped out of Iris, but she hurried inside pushing open the grimy door with her shoulder. She gagged from the smell of stale cigar smoke but bravely continued.

In a tacky office behind smudged glass, she waited for the private investigator to end his phone call. The black letters painted on his glass door were worn and faded and the first letter "h" was almost completely gone. His moniker then became P il Ulrich rather than Phil. She swallowed her doubts, and soon they were talking about Grace. The man seemed skeptical that the child could actually be alive and be her niece, but he was persuaded to take her case by the wad of cash she pulled from her purse and laid on the desk.

"I'm telling you, Charlie." Mae sat at the kitchen table wringing her hands. "It was downright creepy. That man came up to me as I was leaving, showed me a private investigator's card, and said he wanted to ask me a few questions."

"So what did you say?" Charlie asked.

"I told him I was in a huge hurry and walked away. He stood there with his card in his hand and watched me until I pulled out of the parking lot. I'm sure he saw the car and the license plate number."

"Don't worry, Mae." Charlie took her trembling hands in his steady ones. "He might have wanted to ask about something at the hospital. You know, trying to find out about one of the patients. Or doctors."

"Dear, sweet Charlie," Mae said. "You see the best in everything, and I love you for it. But this time I think you're wrong." She trembled again.

"I was afraid this would happen. But we have papers, right? The ones that say she belongs to us."

"We have her birth certificate showing she was born in Cartersville to my sister, Pat, and her husband, Gene. God rest their make-believe souls."

"Well then, if he comes around again and if he's asking questions about Amy, we don't have anything to worry about."

"I hope you're right." Mae's empty-eyed blinking brought out the trouble wrinkles on her forehead. "As long as no one goes looking for Pat. You know that, Charlie."

He nodded. "But we adopted her?"

"Not exactly. Not officially anyway. It costs too much for lawyers. I used our name for her, and there's never been a problem. Until now."

Charlie crossed his arms and leaned back in his chair, silent. At that moment, Amy came running into the kitchen. "Mommy, you're home," she said.

Mae gathered her into her arms and kissed the top of her head. "Yes, sweetheart. Mommy's home now."

Thomas Eikens limped into the boardroom with his right arm in a cast. His face was bruised all along its right side, and he scowled.

The board members had heard about the attack on Thomas. There were complaints and protestations about the lacking police protection and social decline in which safety was becoming more of an issue. It was generally supposed that his attack had been a random act of violence.

Leland cleared his throat and called the meeting to order. "First, let me say, Thomas, we are all sorry for your ordeal. We hope that your assailant is soon caught and brought to justice."

Thomas nodded his acknowledgement, still grim-faced. *Yes, I bet you do, you son-of-a-bitch.*

"Well, you have all of our support," Leland said. "If there's anything you need or anything we can do."

Thomas glowered at him, and the chill of his hatred filled the room.

Leland moved quickly through several agenda items, mostly updates about ongoing projects with a few investment details. Then he opened the floor to discussion of the relocation of the Sara Lee plant.

Marsh Dalton was first to speak. "Gentlemen," he said, "this looks to be a very lucrative opportunity for us. True, our investment is substantial, but cost projections will more than be offset by sale of the land and government subsidy. It was clearly foresight to buy undeveloped property on the far west side of town when we did."

Thomas pounded the table with his left arm and winced from communicated pain to his right arm. "This is just bullshit," he said. "We all know the earmarks are intended for development along the Shawnee River corridor. Why, Marsh, you and Leland and I looked over preliminary drawings of suitable parcels with Senator Greene in your office a few months ago. Now you are zooming ahead with this west side risk with full knowledge of intent to divert government funding from its allocated purpose."

"How dare you?" Thomas continued. His face flushed and his heart raced. "Besides, money isn't in the bank yet. Or is it, Marsh?"

He glared at the dapper banker with the carefully bland expression on his face.

"Well, no," Marsh said. "But Senator Greene has practically guaranteed it, and he's been a reliable source in the past."

Thomas snorted. "He ought to be after all the campaign contributions we made."

Some board members looked nervous.

Leland spoke up. "Look, gentlemen. Our Gilliver House Hotel is in a strategically advantageous location to host commercial interests seeking to operate on the west side. The Sara Lee plant will be at the far western perimeter, and it's only the beginning. I envision an industrial park and residential units plus smaller commercial businesses to fill in greater Tillman west of our hotel."

Now several board members nodded approval and murmured to each other.

Marsh took advantage of the change of tone in the room. "Benefits to the municipality are obvious, gentlemen. Already the town council is drafting an ordinance to place a referendum question for annexation on the ballot for the next election. By that time, plant construction will be underway."

"And we, as property owners, will pay the increased tax levy on all that land," Thomas said.

"Only as undeveloped areas," Marsh said. "The town of Tillman will grow to a city with an influx of territory and capital from tax revenue. It's a win-win situation for us. We all stand to make serious profits from this venture in the next several years." He smiled at the board members seated around the table.

Sympathy for Thomas's position was waning. "If misappropriation of the earmark funds is discovered, there could be legal ramifications, not to mention public relations issues."

"Oh, for Christ's sake, Thomas," Leland stood. "That's why we have company attorneys. By the time that happens, our profits will be rolling in, Tillman's unemployment will drop to nil and the city will be flush with tax revenues for services and even more expansion. It's nothing we can't fix." He looked at his Rolex. "I think we're finished here for now," he said.

Someone moved to adjourn, and it was seconded.

Thomas sat still as the others filed out of the boardroom. He had a sinking feeling that there was far more to these business maneuvers than he knew. For some reason, Leland, and now Marsh, wanted to stop building on the east side. *Now, who is behind the threats? Fix indeed. That son-of-a-bitch.*

"Why do you have to go out tonight?" Donna Sanders asked. "Especially all dressed in black again like you were last night." An acetone smell drifted into the room when she blew lightly onto her freshly painted fingernails, Fire Engine Red.

"Do you expect me to sit here on my ass and wait for that stupid lawyer to get some money? I think it's time to shake him up a bit." Mike said.

"It's been four days since you went to see him. I thought you said you were giving him a week."

"Yeah, but I want him to know I'm serious."

"So, what are you going to do?"

"Relax," Mike said. "Tonight I'm doing a little side job for that banker I told you about. He's always paid damn good. At least you don't complain about the money."

Donna put her hands on her hips. "Be careful, Mike, I don't want anything bad to happen to you."

"Yeah, like then you wouldn't get as much in the settlement," he said.

"Don't be a jerk. I'm the one who saw that asshole."

"Listen, I'm the bad that happens to them," he said and walked out.

Thomas Eikens settled into his favorite chair with a book. But he couldn't concentrate on reading. He was uneasy. *Did I reset the alarm?*

A scraping sound against the window made him hold his breath as he listened. *Must be the wind.* He turned his attention back to the book until it grated on his nerves. Pushing on the chair's edge with his left arm, he struggled to get up without using his bandaged right arm. Hobbling stiffly, he went to the gun case and fumbled with the keys. *Damn left hand.* When he got it open, the lights went out.

A bitter, panicky taste rose in his throat, and he bent to grope around a shelf in the cabinet for his revolver. Standing up, he dropped it and cursed as he fell to his knees to feel for it. Breathing heavily, he pushed himself to his feet. When his eyes adjusted to darkness, he shuffled toward his telephone and picked it up. No dial tone. *Damn. What's going on here? Why in the hell am I being harassed and who's behind it? And that damn cell phone is in my briefcase.*

Touching the wall to guide him, he moved toward the kitchen, toward the back door. *My car keys.* Reaching for the key rack by the door, he saw the silhouette of a man rise outside the door's window from the scant light of a waning moon. He gasped.

The door handle rattled when the man tried to open it. *Locked. Thank God.* But not for long. The door popped open when its frame cracked from the pressure of a crowbar inserted into the jamb.

The man's face was in the shadow. Thomas recognized his voice. He pointed the revolver toward the man and pulled the trigger, but he was so weak his aim went wild.

"You don't need that, mister," the man said. He knocked the gun out of Thomas' weak left hand. Then he grabbed Thomas' left arm and twisted it behind his back.

Damn consistent bastard. Thomas pressed his lips together to keep from screaming.

The man shoved him to the floor and kicked him. Thomas refused to cry out. "From what I hear, you didn't get the message last time," he said.

"Who are you? What do you want?" Thomas asked. The scent of his own fear mixed with the smell of stale beer, nauseating him.

"Never mind that, gramps," the man said as he grabbed Thomas' shirt, pulling him to a sitting position before he punched him in the face. Thomas fell back. His head bounced on the parquet kitchen floor before he lost all consciousness.

Leland drummed his fingers on the table as he downed the last of his martini. *Just like a damned board meeting.* He held up his empty glass to signal a waiter for a refill.

Brian hurried to the table at the club and slid quickly into a chair across from Leland. "Sorry I'm late," he said. "It was something of an emergency."

Leland frowned. "I don't care what it was. You keep me waiting for lunch and don't take my phone calls." He paused to point a finger at Brian. "For the money I'm paying you, I expect better treatment," he said. "Not to mention results. What the hell is going on?"

Brian paused. The waiter put his customary scotch in front of him. "It doesn't mean we're–I'm– not working on your project," he said.

"My project!" Leland's voice boomed, causing other diners to look in his direction. He lowered his voice to a menacing growl. "My project, you're damn right, Brian. But don't forget you're in it all the way too. We stand to make a fortune."

"I haven't forgotten. In fact, I've some news for you."

"Let's have it," Leland said. "It's about time."

"There's been a breakthrough in the real estate tangle. It's not 100% tied down yet."

"So?" Leland leaned forward.

"So, I think you'll be surprised." Brian picked up a menu he never used.

"Give it up, man. I don't like playing games. Unless I control them."

"All paper trails seem to lead to a trust fund, a rather large and complex one. The fund is a major investor in some GillRich Construction matters. But not on the west side."

Leland's eyebrows rose. "So, somebody on the board, maybe, has that land. Hmm." He sat back. "Wonder who it is? Thomas Eikens?

He won't back down from his position, even in the hospital. Poor dumb bastard."

"I don't think so," Brian said, "though he might be involved since he's usually tight with someone else on the board."

"Marsh?" Leland was incredulous. "He is opposed to an east side venture." Realization rose within him. "Unless he wants to throw us off so he can jump on future development himself."

"I doubt it. It looks like he's held that land in trust for a good forty years or more."

"So he's a slum lord too." Leland mused in silence for a few minutes.

"That changes things, doesn't it?" Brian asked.

"Only temporarily, my boy. It makes it more interesting. There must be some reason Marsh wanted to keep it hidden. When we discover that, he might be persuaded to sell, quietly and cheaply of course. Unless he doesn't cooperate."

Brian didn't respond. Both men cut into their steaks and finished their meals in silence.

8

Acceleration

"They're all different, but all the same, Mommy, look," Amy said. She skipped along the paving bricks between blooming spring borders at the municipal park.

Mae gazed at mass plantings of brightly colored tulips and golden daffodils. "All the same?" she asked.

"All flowers," Amy said as she crouched to sniff a cream-colored hyacinth. "Ooh, this smells good, Mommy. Come see."

Mae hurried to her side and breathed in the heady sweet scent of the hyacinths. Amy danced ahead of her along the path, stopping to stick her nose into every pretty flower she could. *She's as delightful as this beautiful spring day.* Mae turned to admire a screen of forsythia bushes in bloom.

Along the path toward Amy her vision froze. Her heart hammered and her chest tightened. She sprinted to where Amy was talking to a man who had stooped to Amy's eye level. He was holding a flower out to her.

Mae grabbed Amy's hand. She recognized the private investigator who had stopped her when she left work. "How dare you!" she shouted. "How dare you bother my child?"

"But ma'am…"

"Mommy," Amy said as Mae pulled her away and walked quickly in the other direction. "That man picked a flower. You told me we couldn't pick flowers."

"How many times have I told you not to talk to strangers?" Mae said between gritted teeth.

"But Mommy, he wanted to give me a flower," Amy said in protest. "He called me a pretty girl."

"We're leaving now," Mae said, picking up her pace. She was afraid to look behind her.

At home, Mae calmed herself by going through the motions of making a pot of chamomile tea. The fragrance soothed her frayed nerves. Amy chattered to Charlie about pretty flowers and the playground she had seen there.

"Let's go back, Daddy," she said. "But don't pick flowers, no, no."

Mae took a deep breath. "Amy, go play with Dolly for a while before lunch," she said. "I want to talk to Daddy now."

Amy crossed her arms over her little chest in a stubborn gesture. "I want to go to the playground."

"Not now, honey." Mae fought to control jittery hands. "Daddy will play with you later."

"Go on," Charlie said, patting Amy gently on the behind.

She pouted for a moment then said, "Okay, but you promised, Daddy."

Charlie laughed.

When Amy was busy at the toy box, Mae poured tea. The two cups rattled and clacked together as she carried them to the worn table and sat across from her husband.

"He's following us, Charlie," she said. "It's the same man. I'm sure of it."

"What happened?" he asked.

"He was talking to Amy and tried to give her a flower. I looked away for only a minute, I swear, Charlie, and there he was."

"Did he touch her? Maybe this guy's a kidnapper." Charlie sounded alarmed.

"He didn't have a chance. I got there and pulled her away from him as fast as I could."

Charlie looked down into his cup. "Are you sure, Mae? Are you sure it's the same man?

Maybe it was, you know, random, a coincidence, or you're being, what's the word? Para–"

"Paranoid," Mae said. "No, I'm not imagining this, Charlie." Mae pushed her hair back and reached for his hand. "It was no coincidence. I'm so scared."

Charlie squeezed her hand. "Well, you didn't talk to him, did you? He might go away."

Mae's eyes misted. "No, I don't think so, honey. There's something else." She leveled her gaze at him. "In the car, on the way home, Amy told me he called her Grace."

Hard to believe Amy's going to be in second grade next year. Charlie stuffed his hands into the pockets of his jeans jacket and whistled as he walked around the corner. *This is the way life's supposed to be.*

He stopped in front of Tillman Elementary where other parents milled about, waiting to meet their children. He knew the other parents by sight if not by name, and they made amiable small talk. "Beautiful spring day. Still a little cool."

The bell rang, and school doors flew open as children spilled outside. Charlie's heart leapt with pride when he saw Amy. She ran to him, laughing and chattering about her day. He hugged her, then held her hand while they walked away.

In a black SUV parked unobtrusively among minivans, other SUV's and cars waiting outside, Sylvia sat next to the private investigator. At the sound of whistling through her partially lowered window, she recognized Charlie walking toward the school.

"That's him. That's who I saw in the doctor's office," she said to the private investigator sitting behind the wheel. Something else seemed familiar about him but she couldn't place it.

When Amy ran to Charlie and they started walking back, Sylvia watched every move, captivated, until they turned the corner out of sight.

"It's my niece. I'm positive. That man stole my sister's daughter."

The investigator talked in a drawl. "Now, ma'am. If I got the story right, she died as a little baby in a train wreck something like almost seven years ago. I don't mind taking your money, see, but how can you prove it?"

"First of all, her remains were never found at the wreckage."

He nodded. "That's understandable. It was a huge explosion, and she was a tiny one. There might never be an answer to that."

"The proof just walked away. That's all I need to know. My husband's an attorney, and I'm sure he'll know what I can do."

The investigator scratched his chin for a moment. "Now as far as that goes, ma'am," he said. "Do you mean what you can do legally?"

Sylvia sipped her morning coffee as she read the newspaper. "Brian," she asked, "did you know about the break in at Thomas Eiken's house two nights ago?"

"No." Brian stopped eating his breakfast and blotted his mouth with a napkin.

"His cleaning lady found him lying unconscious on his kitchen floor yesterday morning. He's in the hospital."

"Did they take anything?" Brian asked.

"Yes, police say robbery was the motive. They're not sure what else was taken, but they noticed his guns were missing."

"Sounds like they were after him."

"Why would you say that?"

"No reason." Brian chewed his toast. "Did he have his alarm on?"

"I guess not, but it's close to here, you know, and I'm frightened by the thought of robberies in this part of town."

"Probably some low life from the east side."

"It doesn't matter where he's from," Sylvia said. "I'm calling the security service today to check our system."

"Good idea," Brian brushed crumbs from his hands. He stood. "In fact, call them this morning. We don't want to take any chances."

Sylvia turned back to reading the paper. "Okay," she said.

"I mean it, Sylvia. It would be terrible to go through something like old Eikens went through. So promise me you'll call right away."

Sylvia put down the newspaper. Her husband was pale and appeared serious.

"Okay, I said. What's the matter, Brian?"

He leaned over to kiss her cheek. "Work's on my mind, that's all, darling," he said. "I'm off."

He's more upset about this than I am.

Sylvia ambled from room to room in her large, empty house. Brian was working late again, and it was Marianna's night off. Sylvia felt restless.

She clicked on the television but nothing interested her. She tossed down the remote control right before she heard an unusual rattling noise. At the alarm box in the front hallway, she breathed an inaudible sigh. It was still a safe and solid red.

Silly. Then she heard it again, louder this time and closer. It was coming from the front of the house.

She pressed the speed-dial button on the land line she had programmed for the police department.

"Tillman police," the dispatcher answered.

"This is Mrs.–" The line went dead. An instant later the house went dark. Sylvia ran back to the front hallway. The face of the alarm control was glowing green. A second later, it flashed red when the battery backup engaged. *But it won't notify the police department if the phone lines are cut!*

What do I do now? Sylvia held her breath as she strained to listen. No more rattling, but now a loud scraping noise alongside the house made her jump. *Upstairs?* She raced toward the front stairway, slipping as she missed her first attempt at grabbing the banister in the dark. She landed hard on her left knee and bit her tongue. Tears of rage and pain sprang to her eyes, but she pushed herself, scrambling upstairs and swallowing back the metallic taste of blood in her mouth.

Sylvia was running along the hallway toward the master bedroom when a loud crash and breaking glass came from a guest bedroom. She slammed and locked her door, leaning against it panting. Everything was quiet.

Even before her vision became accustomed to darkness, she crossed to her closet and fumbled for a shoebox on the top shelf. *Why, oh why, didn't I think of this before?* She groped for the pearl handle of a lady pistol, a Chief Special Air Weight her father had given her twenty years ago. *I haven't touched this in years. Where are the bullets?*

Sylvia wrenched the shoebox off the shelf and it fell, spilling bullets across the floor. *Damn. What now?* She dropped down and crawled around, searching for bullets. Then her throat started to burn and her eyes watered. The smell was sickly, cloying bitterness. *Tear gas?* She wasn't sure but she started coughing uncontrollably while she got up and staggered to the window. Her arms felt heavy and leaden when she pushed open the lock. As soon as she got it opened, she gulped fresh air, clearing her head.

Reaching back toward her dresser, she found her purse, fumbled inside for the cell phone, and punched *911*. Then, listening for any sound over her thrumming pulse, all was silent until sirens screamed nearby. *Thank God.*

Downstairs, police called her name as they tromped through the rooms. She was too paralyzed with fear to move. *What if he's still up here?* She shivered in the cool spring air from the open window.

Startled, she jumped when the doorknob rattled as someone tried to open the door. Then there was a pounding. "Tillman Police, Mrs. Boggs, are you in there?"

Sylvia was shaking so hard she could barely unlock the door. She finally opened it to see two policemen in gas masks. They helped her downstairs, away from the fumes.

"Are you okay, Mrs. Boggs?" Sergeant Andrews sat her down on the couch and handed her a glass of water.

"What happened?" Sylvia felt dizzy.

"We have a team on the way to gather evidence upstairs and will be able to tell you more then. It looks like someone broke in through one of your bedroom windows and set off a tear gas grenade, and then came downstairs to leave."

"Downstairs?" Sylvia looked around in the dimness. She shook off a wave of nausea. "How did you get in?"

"The front door was wide open, ma'am."

"It couldn't be. I locked all the doors." Sylvia was trembling again.

"Yes ma'am," Andrews was both patient and polite. "That's where we figure the intruder went out. All other doors and windows downstairs are locked. We called the power company, so they should have your lights on soon."

"Who? Why?" Sylvia put her head in her hands.

"We have a witness–one of your neighbors saw a shadowy figure in front of your shrubbery. He came over to tell us when he heard sirens and saw police cars. It might have been the suspect. We called your husband's office too. He should be here any minute so try to relax."

Sylvia needed to vomit, but she swallowed to keep it down. She wrapped herself in an afghan she kept on the couch: Her thoughts swirled. Her head was pounding. *This is crazy. Who'd want to hurt me? It must have been a burglar. But tear gas?*

Brian burst into the room and ran to her. "Oh my God, Sylvia," he said. "Sergeant Andrews told me everything. Are you hurt?"

She opened her mouth to tell him about the throbbing pain in her left knee, beginning to swell, but the lights came on at that moment. The large oil portrait of Brian and her on their wedding day had been slashed and ripped to shredded hanging tatters. Brian's face went white. Sylvia screamed.

9

Danger

Nora Noble loved her new job as a Teacher's Assistant at Tillman Elementary. Her heels clacked like falling acorns on the sidewalk as she hurried to the school's big doors, breathing deeply the musky scent of fresh autumn.

In the classroom, bright with primary colors, she conferred with the teacher and set up for the day's lessons. Glancing outside, she saw children arriving, running around the schoolyard, many with their parents still watching from their cars or beyond the gate.

She wasn't supposed to have favorites, but she smiled when she saw Amy Jericho walking hand-in-hand with her father. *That little girl is bright as a penny.* Nora laughed at her own thoughts and returned to her task. Soon, she went outside to greet the children lining up with their classmates to file inside when the arrival bell rang.

Second graders still loved their teachers and clustered around Nora eagerly. She gathered them to her like chicks to a hen. She counted twenty-nine bright faces before leading them into an old-fashioned cloakroom to hang up their jackets or sweaters and deposit their lunch boxes.

Once the students were settled at their desks, the teacher, Mrs. Isaac, started their lessons with a spelling review. Nora checked off the daily computer attendance record. It was too early in the school year for many absences–cold and flu season had not yet begun. But Nora recorded twenty-nine out of thirty. Amy Jericho was absent.

That's funny. I saw her. And her dad.

Later, while children were busy with art projects, Nora mentioned the discrepancy.

Mrs. Isaac wrinkled her nose, a nervous habit. "I hope she's okay. Amy's off to a great start this year."

"The strange thing is I saw her father too," Nora said. "So why would he have walked her to school if she was ill?"

"The office compiles our attendance records for their master list," Mrs. Isaac said. "In this case, I think we should draw Amy's absence to their attention."

Going through her workday motions, Mae hummed and sung an old Beatles song under her breath. *"Love is real. Real is love."* She adjusted pillows and I.V. needles with deft competence; pausing to say a silent prayer over the sickest little patients she attended.

Her supervisor was a gruff-looking but tenderhearted woman named Flora. Mae had always liked her, partly because of their mutual professional respect and their shared love of children.

Flora was waiting when Mae finished her first visit. There were beads of perspiration on Flora's top lip and heavy breathing, as if she'd run throughout the wing. Flora grasped Mae's elbow.

"Honey, there's a police officer waiting for you in the administrator's office downstairs," she said. "Better hurry now. I'll take over for you here." Flora took the patient's charts from Mae's arms.

Mae's stomach lurched. "What is it?" she asked.

"It's about Amy, honey. She didn't show up at school," Flora said. "You go on now."

Mae was already sprinting toward the elevators. She saw both cars were at ground level and griped with panic, pushed open the stairwell door. Stumbling and jerking, she ran downstairs, afraid to think.

The CEO of Mercy Hospital was a kindly old man who had made a point to get to know the staff and speak to them by name. "Mae, this is Sergeant Andrews," he said, "of the Tillman Police."

"Mae Jericho?" Andrews asked as he shook Mae's shaky hand.

Mae nodded. "My daughter? Flora said Amy didn't go to school? I don't understand. Where's Charlie? Did you talk to my husband?"

"Ordinarily, Mrs. Jericho," Andrews said, "a second grader not showing up for school would not be a police matter. But we're following up because a Teacher's Assistant by the name of Nora Noble said she saw both your daughter and your husband at the schoolyard only moments before the opening bell."

"That sounds right," Mae said. "Charlie always walks Amy to school and one of us is always there to pick her up."

"But when the children lined up to come into the classroom, there was no Amy.

Mrs. Noble reported it to the office and they called your husband. There was no answer."

Is he saying both my daughter and my husband are missing? Mae shook her head. It was incomprehensible.

Andrews asked Mae to sit down, and her stomach plummeted as she bent her wobbling knees to slide into a chair next to the police officer. "It's unusual," he said, "but both Mrs. Noble and Amy's teacher, Mrs. Isaac, were concerned so they followed up. The office called us."

Mae began wringing her hands. *What on earth is he saying?*

"No one is at your house," he said. "Everything seems to be in order though. No break in or signs of one evident from the perimeter check. This still would not have been a police matter, necessarily, but the mother of one of Amy's classmates called to report a possible abduction."

Mae's heart beat faster and trickles of perspiration pooled on her scalp.

Andrews continued. "On her way back to her car after walking her daughter to the schoolyard, Mrs. Folger happened to look along a side street, around the corner from the playground. She saw Mr. Jericho being shoved into a burgundy-colored van parked there.

"She recognized Charlie because her daughter had invited Amy to play at their house and Charlie had come to get her."

"Amy?" Mae's voice was barely a whisper.

"Mrs. Folger didn't see Amy, but Mrs. Noble remembered seeing her from her classroom window. So, I have to ask you, Mrs. Jericho, have you noticed anything out of the ordinary lately or do you know of anyone who would want to possibly hurt your husband or your daughter?"

By this time, Mae's tears were sliding down her cheeks. *This can't be happening.* The kindly administrator brought her a glass of water and patted her shoulder.

She told Sergeant Andrews of her encounter with the private investigator and Amy at the park, briefly, hoping her voice belied no trace of guilt. *I should have seen this coming. But Charlie too?*

Andrews had written in a small notebook before standing to shake the administrator's hand. He turned to Mae.

"We have a description of the van and are tracing it now. If you can think of anything else that might help us find your family, call me." He handed her a business card.

"Sergeant," she asked, "you said Mrs. Folger only saw Charlie, not Amy. Maybe Amy ran away and is looking for her Daddy. Or coming here?" Mae bit her bottom lip.

"Oh, yes, there's another thing, Mrs. Jericho," he said. "We found this on the street where the van was parked." He pulled something from a bag sitting on the floor.

"Does this belong to Amy?"

It was the sweater she herself knitted and her vision thoroughly blurred before she fainted.

The cold metal of the van's cargo area reverberated with a dull thud when Charlie's cheek slammed against it. Someone slapped a piece of duct tape over his mouth. He bit his tongue. For a brief moment he feared he would strangle in his own blood, until another fear took over. Amy sobbing.

He struggled to turn toward her, but a blindfold was tied around his head, over his eyes. Too tight. His head throbbed.

His arms were tied behind his back, at the elbows and at the wrists, making it impossible for him to use them as leverage to push himself up. His shoulders cramped and confusion swirled through his thoughts. *What's going on? What have I done? Amy! Amy! My little angel. Daddy is here!* He twisted and squirmed to get himself free until a sharp pain from a kick in his ribs stopped him. He gasped and lay still, head swimming in agony and fear. *Daddy is helpless, Amy, helpless, helpless . . . helpless.*

Charlie sensed himself drifting but didn't want to slide into unconsciousness for Amy's sake. He couldn't move, see or speak, but he could still hear. The van's engine started and thumped into gear. From his position on the bare metal floor the sound of the tires against the pavement roared. He concentrated on listening for voices of his captors. Exhaust fumes crept over his face, pressed against the thin bottom of the van.

Amy sobbed softly. It gave him a strange kind of comfort. *She's still alive!* Surging anger and rage were unfamiliar emotions but now they ricocheted through him and his adrenaline swelled. He could spring into action as soon as he was untied. If they untied him. Hatred seized him. *If they touch Amy, they're dead!*

His cheek bounced against the floor of the van as it picked up speed. *Where are we going?* He strained to hear the voices.

It sounded like two men, both speaking low, but some of the words were audible. "Hurt … strip mine."

They are taking us away from Tillman, to the west. There's an old gravel pit far beyond the plains above the river bluffs. What the hell? We could be lost for days out there. Then something worse came to Charlie's mind. *Oh no, oh no.* He shook with fear.

The van came to an abrupt stop. His captors jumped out and opened the side door. They dragged him through the cargo door and pushed him hard. He landed on his knees, rocks cutting the soft fabric of his jeans. Someone shoved him and he fell face-first onto the ground. A third voice. *A woman? Foreign sounding?*

Amy was whimpering then crying, "Daddy! Daddy! Don't hurt Daddy!"

"Shut up kid," a man said. Amy screamed, and Charlie stiffened, stretching against his constraints.

"Let's get this over with," a man said. The woman's voice said something he didn't understand to a man who responded in the same language. Amy's crying was coming from farther away. A car door slammed.

Are they going to kill me now? Or leave me here? "Amy! Amy!" he screamed soundlessly until his throat ached. Someone kicked him in the ribs again, and he gasped for breath.

The sliding thunk of the side van door closing was quickly followed by sounds of gravel crunching under tires. *They're leaving.*

Charlie pushed himself up. Every muscle in his body shuddered. The sharp rocks helped him loosen the ties around his hands. He strained, pulled a hand free and ripped the blindfold from his head, scratching his cheek with his own fingernails in his haste. With his other hand he ripped duct tape from his mouth and screamed.

His eyes adjusted to the light in time to see a black SUV and a burgundy van speeding away. He ran after them but his legs were so weak that he stumbled to his knees after a few steps. He choked back tears. "Amy! Amy!"

Something gave him hope, though, as he sat crying and gasping for breath on hard gravel-covered ground. Charlie had seen the license numbers.

Amy trembled and sucked in her breath. The car's abrupt turn as it accelerated threw her across the back seat into the side door headfirst. She cried out. Someone's hands, the woman's, grasped her, pulling her upright again. There was no comfort in her touch, and Amy's tears wet the kerchief tied tight around her eyes.

"Where am I? Who are you? What did you do to Daddy?"

The woman said something in words Amy didn't understand, but she heard sternness in the hard voiced reprimand. Still, she tried again. "Where are you taking me? I want my Daddy!"

Her head flew backward from the force of the slap across her face. She wailed. Her shoulders shook with sobs.

A man talked loudly to the woman, and the woman answered. Amy became aware of the woman's movements right before a strange odor filled the car and a cloth was pressed to her face, covering her nose and mouth. She squirmed to pull away from it but not in time.

Evening shadows soaked the briskly utilitarian office in somber shades of gray and purple. Sergeant Andrews sat opposite a forlorn couple. Charlie was battered and desperate-looking. His face was bruised, and the skin next to his mouth was red and blistery where the duct tape had been ripped off. Claw marks from fingernails were clearly visible on his cheek above his beard.

Mae was overcome with intermittent crying. Neither had been very forthcoming with details of their daughter's abduction, but then, Andrews supposed, they had told him what they knew.

"Now, Mr. Jericho," he said. "Just so I have the details correct, will you tell me everything you can remember about what happened?"

Charlie vibrated with pent-up energy; he stood and paced. "Sergeant, sir, you have to help us find Amy. We don't know what to do. Nothing like this has ever happened to us."

"That's what I'm doing. Now, from the beginning, please."

Andrews perceived Mae Jericho's nervousness when her husband talked. *Hell, I don't blame her. I guess I'd be the same way if my kid had been grabbed.*

Charlie said, "I always walk to school with Amy."

"Always? Isn't that a long walk for a second-grader? And in all kinds of weather?"

"What difference does it make?" Mae asked, her face a swollen aftermath of crying. "I mean, in finding our daughter now."

"I'm trying to picture the pattern, Mrs. Jericho," Andrews said. "If Charlie and Amy walk together every day, at the same time, someone could have observed their habit which made it easier to predict and therefore plan the..." Andrews hesitated as he searched for the right word. "Abduction."

Charlie looked back and forth from Mae to him. "You see, I can't dr—"

"You don't drive? Even in bad weather?"

"I take the car to work, at the hospital," Mae said.

Andrews nodded. "Go on," he said to Charlie.

"Well, today I walked her to school, like always, and she was talking to her friends in the school yard. She went to line up with other children in her class when the first bell rang, so I started walking home."

Charlie sat down, looking at his hands. "By God, if they hurt her, I'll kill them!"

Mae burst into tears.

"Don't even think of threats like that, Jericho. You can only get yourself and your family in more trouble that way. It's our job to catch them and get your daughter back."

Charlie lifted his head and stared into Andrews' eyes for a long moment. His flat, blue eyes returned the stare, hoping Charlie got the message about not attempting to track kidnappers on his own. But Andrews had trouble reading him. *Wonder what's behind that look, so feral and wild?* Charlie appeared so mild-mannered until now.

"Tell him what happened next, Charlie," Mae said, touching Charlie's arm gently.

Charlie stood and paced again. "After I went around the corner by the playground, I stopped to catch my breath. The leaves on the trees were just turning."

"Real fast, a couple of guys jumped out of a dark red van and twisted my arms behind me, slapped duct tape over my mouth and a blindfold over my eyes. I kicked at them. One shouted, but I didn't understand what he said. I struggled. They dragged me into the van and tied my arms behind me, then threw me onto the floor. I landed on the side of my face, all the time in a kind of shock. Then the van door opened and closed again and a child's voice cried. It was Amy!"

Mae put her hands over her face.

"They kicked me in the ribs when I struggled to get up so I lay still after that, with my ear pressed against the floor, listening to figure out where we were going." Now Charlie cried, distressed and unabashed. "I couldn't help her! I couldn't protect my little girl."

Andrews waited. Patience was necessary in these kinds of cases. Mae grasped Charlie's hand and held it until he composed himself. Presently, Charlie took some tissues to blow his nose, and in a halting voice, spoke again.

"They were going to kill me. The van moved so fast it had to be going out of town. When it stopped without warning, I was on the ground."

Charlie's tears were like liquid pools of poison. "Amy was calling me. A car door slammed..." He shuddered and wrapped his arms around his body. "They were gone, Sergeant, and I tried to chase them..." Charlie hung his head.

"Anything else?" Andrews asked after a time had passed.

Charlie raised his eyes. "Yes!" he said. "I got the numbers on their license plates."

Mae gnashed her teeth on the way home. A tiny hole of emptiness inside her, in the mysterious location of her infertile womb, was growing, and a void would soon engulf her. She would cease to be. Whoever stole Amy stole Mae's identity. She was nothing if not a mother.

Mae glanced sideways at Charlie, pitiful in his grief, but she was repulsed. *How could I ever have loved him? He lost our daughter! It's his fault Amy's gone. So what if he found Amy in the first place?*

"I'll bet that man had something to do with it," she said, now tearless. Her voice rose in a crescendo of anger. "That man who talked to me outside of work and who gave Amy a flower at the park. Somebody knows, Charlie. I told you we should leave."

Charlie sounded wearier than ever when he sighed deeply before he spoke. "How could we, Mae? We talked about it. There's no money."

Mae suppressed a pang of tenderness for Charlie, continuing to feed her mental blame toward him. "Money doesn't mean anything to me without Amy," she said.

"You're right. You're always right. Running away might have kept us safe. Kept Amy with us."

"It would've been pro-active. Something we could do. It might've worked." Mae began to grind her teeth again.

"What about our life here? Besides we don't even know if that man had anything to do with it."

"We had a life, Charlie," Mae said as she pulled into their gravel driveway. The forlorn-looking silhouette of the unlit house unleashed her sorrow. The dark sister of her soul was rising up in her, full of many shadings of rejection, fear, indignity, distress and loneliness. She slumped forward with her forehead against the steering wheel and cried.

Charlie moved to put his arm around her, but she pushed him away.

10

Surprises

Crystal hurried along the dusky sidewalk into the police station. She was shown directly to Sergeant Andrews' office where he was waiting for her.

He rose and shook her hand. "Ms. Winston," he said, pulling out a chair for her, "would you like a cup of coffee?"

"No th-thank you," Crystal stammered. Her stomach felt tight and her cold fingers fidgeted.

"What can we do for you?" Andrews asked.

"Well, may not be anything to this," she said. "But I know Mae Jericho, pretty well. We work together."

"Go on."

"See, I know her little girl, Amy, was taken, or so I heard. Anyway, she's missing." Crystal paused to fish a tissue out of her purse but held it only to the cold tip of her nose. "I hope she's okay because she's a darling little girl. A joy to be around."

"Yes, we hope she's okay too, but—"

"I'm not sure she's Mae's child! Sorry, I blurted that out, but that's why I came. See, I've worked with Mae for a long time and she'd never said she had a sister, or any family for that matter." Crystal blew her nose.

Andrews waited.

"She probably doesn't remember, or I'm sure she doesn't, but anyway, one time she told me she didn't have anyone, and in fact, she was raised by a foster family. So, when she told me her little baby, Amy, was her sick sister's child..."

"Did you question her about it?"

"Not really. I said something about the fact I didn't know she had a sister, but she shrugged. She didn't explain and I didn't ask her because, to tell the truth, I was happy for her because, you know," Crystal looked down. "She and Charlie can't, or I mean, they lost..."

Andrews responded slowly. "Ms. Winston, are you saying that Mae and Charlie Jericho have a child who isn't theirs or a relative's? Are you saying the child is a foundling or belongs to someone else?"

Crystal shook her head and choked back tears. "No. Maybe I shouldn't have even come. But Sergeant, if that precious little girl really does belong to someone else, I know they'd want her. And why would someone take her? Mae and Charlie have no money."

Andrews rubbed his chin. "Is there anything else that makes you think maybe their little girl isn't who they say she is?"

"No sir, except, except something doesn't seem right. The way Mae talks about her and the way Charlie stays home with her all the time. Don't get me wrong, I like Mae and Charlie for that matter, but it seems like they're hiding something."

Andrews stood. "Thank you, Ms. Winston. I'll look into it and take what you've said into consideration. There's one more question I have for you, though. If it comes to it, would you testify in court about what you told me?"

Crystal dabbed her eyes with the crumpled tissue and nodded. "Yes, Sergeant. Yes, if it comes to that."

Smoke curled upward in a blue-gray cloud from the woman's cigarette. It mingled with dingy soot on the concrete block walls and settled on cobwebs clinging to the ceiling and draped across corners.

A man muttered as he paced back and forth in the tiny room, pausing only once to regard the frightened child, hands bound behind her back, mouth covered with a ragged strip of duct tape. The girl shivered as a cockroach crawled toward her and then fled when she moved her foot.

"What if they don't come up with the money?" he asked in Russian.

The woman laughed before she spewed forth a string of words in the same language. "Of course they will, you idiot. We know that woman wants this one." She gestured toward Amy. "If they don't cooperate, we know where we can sell her." She stamped out her cigarette and laughed again.

The man pulled a handkerchief from his pants pocket and wiped sweat from his forehead. "You better be right this time, Elena," he said.

The woman spat her cynical laugh yet again. She reached for another cigarette from a pack lying on the rickety table next to her. She struck a match on the wooden tabletop and smiled at him while a cell phone lying next to the ashtray began to vibrate and buzz.

Sylvia sat immobile like a sentry staring at the space on her living room wall that once held a wedding portrait of Brian and her. Now the walls had been repainted and the space filled with an abstract in oil. Expensive but nondescript. *How did it come to this?*

To her left sat Sergeant Andrews and another police officer, writing in a notebook. Other officers and police technicians moved in the background, installing surveillance equipment and listening devices on her phone. Brian stood next to her, his expression punctured.

"So, let me get this right, Mrs. Boggs," Andrews asked. "You've received a ransom demand for someone else's child?"

Sylvia nodded, swallowing hard to control her voice. "The child is my niece, as I told you, Sergeant Andrews. Since her parents are both deceased, that would make her my child, wouldn't it? I'm her only living relative." She crossed her arms and gripped her elbows to steady herself. *Why don't they rescue Grace? We can sort out the truth later.*

Andrews raised an eyebrow. "Well, the Jericho's have reported their daughter taken yesterday. In fact, the father was abducted too, at the same time, and then released outside of town. From everything we know so far, it could be the same child. Why are you getting a ransom note for their daughter?"

Sylvia jumped up to face the officers. "That man is not her father. I've told you. He's a kidnapper too, probably in on this ransom thing because he needs money." Hot tears overflowed her eyes. Her voice shook. "For God's sake, just find her!"

Brian finally spoke; draping his arm around Sylvia's shaking shoulders, as if to tamp down her anger. "Now you've upset my wife," he said in his practical, lawyerly tone. "We've already explained this. Those people, Jericho and his wife, are criminals, and if we have to see it proved in court, we will. Please, let's quit wasting time and save that child."

Andrews told the other officer. "Bring in the P.I."

Charlie wandered around his house, inside and out, with no apparent purpose. He didn't see shabbiness intruding on neat orderliness. Already clean, everything was re-cleaned and Charlie's tidiness grew from habit to compulsion, as if this perceived perfection would change things. As if it would bring Amy back.

He found Mae sitting in Amy's room, clutching a doll. Their conversations were perfunctory, and she had relinquished the habit of reading the newspaper to him, teaching him to read. He felt truly bereft–a man adrift on an ice flow connected by only a thin cord that might soon become so long it would be impossible to pull him back.

So often he telephoned the police station, he became a person of interest in the case of the missing child. Mae's silent coldness bewildered him, and he kept searching for a spark of their old love in her vacant eyes.

"She's really gone, Charlie," Mae whispered when he asked her if she read anything about it in the newspaper, if she knew anything else he didn't know. "That policeman, Sergeant Andrews, has been asking some strange questions lately. He seems to think she's not ours, that we are lying or not telling the whole truth. But she is ours, Charlie." Mae fixed a fierce gaze on Charlie, but her voice was soft. "She was a gift from God. He meant for us to have her."

"Mae," Charlie said, "maybe we should tell the truth. You know that's what I've always thought. The truth about how we found her, I mean."

"You can't be serious! After all these years, you still think she belongs to somebody else.

Well, I'll tell you something, Charlie Jericho, she is our child and that's that. Don't even think anything else, hear me?" Mae was shouting now.

"Mae, I'll do whatever you say if you think it's right, and if it will make it be like it was between us."

"It never will until we get Amy back. You lost her, now you better find her or else we have nothing here. And we never will."

Charlie's throat closed around a cold lump, preventing him from speaking. He hugged himself as he turned away from his wife and another truth he didn't want to see. *She has never really loved me.*

Leland drummed his fingertips on the table. *Where the hell is he?* He downed his martini in a single gulp and grimaced from the bitter comfort of it.

These moments of waiting for Brian, he realized, were becoming more frequent and lengthy. *By God, he's avoiding me! I'm the client, power broker, chairman of the board of GillRich here. Who does he think he is?* Leland swiveled in his chair and looked toward the door for the third time in five minutes.

Brian arrived, white-faced and perspiring. He offered no explanation for being late but slid into his chair and slammed back the scotch waiting there for him. Leland glared at him.

"Before you say anything," Brian said, holding up his palms. "You must hear about Grace."

At the mention of her name, Leland straightened in his chair and squinted at Brian. "Well, spit it out then. I thought you were finally going to have some news for me on the east side project, but, of course, Grace…"

"She's been kidnapped, I mean, kidnapped again. A second time."

"How the hell can that be?" Leland's voice boomed as he stood with such force he knocked over his chair.

All conversation in the club restaurant ceased, and everyone stared at the obvious breach of protocol. Brian looked around, then down at the tablecloth; he retrieved a monogrammed handkerchief from his jacket pocket and blotted his perspiring forehead.

Leland was oblivious to his surroundings or to embarrassment. He glowered at Brian, his irritation escalating. "Don't think you can play games with me, Boggs," he said, leaning forward with both hands flat on the table. In a lower voice he said, "You'd better start making sense real fast. I'm in no mood to be jerked around today. Especially when it comes to news of my granddaughter."

Brian said "Let's get out of here." He rushed to the exit with Leland only one step away. As the door eased shut, a buzz of voices erupted behind it.

In an alcove shaded by a stately poplar a few feet from the club's entrance, Leland grasped Brian's elbow with a determined grip. He saw panic flash in Brian's eyes before the lawyer composed his practiced features. Leland waited, staring into the younger man's eyes until Brian shifted his gaze sideways and down. *He's getting ready to lie to me.*

Brian coughed and blotted his face with his handkerchief again. "She's alive, Leland. Or at least she was."

"Speak plainly."

"I'm sure of it. Sylvia has convinced me. Someone is demanding a ransom for her. From us!"

Leland slumped onto the stone bench next to them in the alcove. "You'd better start at the beginning," he said. "Why would someone be asking for a ransom from you? How can you be sure it's Grace? Where is she?"

A police car rolled through the parking lot. "This is not the place."

"Okay," Leland said. He gathered himself to a standing position though his heart pounded and his face felt clammy. He nodded toward the police officer watching them as he trolled past. "Let's go for a ride. We can talk in the car."

They got into Leland's sedan and glided out of the parking lot, turning east. They rode in silence for some minutes before Leland cleared his throat and asked, "How long have you known Grace is alive?"

"We never did really know it. Until now, I mean." Brian sighed. "Sylvia has suspected it for a while. She saw the girl a few times and said she was exactly like Lisa at that age. She was so confident she hired a P.I. to identify the child. A man by the name of Philip Ulrich."

Leland nodded and fixed his gaze at the road as he headed out of town toward the river. "I know him. Go on."

"It was a harmless obsession, a preoccupation with ghosts. Possibly because of her lingering grief. But," he shrugged. "I'm no psychologist. I played along, hoping she would abandon the idea."

"Damn it, man." Leland pounded his fist against the steering wheel. "Get to the point!"

"I am," Brian said. "Starting at the beginning, like you suggested. Anyway, turns out the P.I.–Ulrich–found out who the parents, or alleged parents, of the little girl are and managed to actually talk to them. Far as I know, he was in the process of securing some positive I.D., like something we could use to determine a match for DNA. Of course, hers would be similar to Sylvia's, as Lisa's sister and yours, as Ben's father."

Leland pulled into the gravel driveway of the river cabin that had belonged to his former partner, John Gilliver. He had often been there and had used it for personal meetings from time to time. "Look, Brian," he said, turning to face him. "Skip the elementary stuff. What's happened to Grace?"

They got out and Brian followed Leland to the cabin's back door. With a deft movement, Leland unlocked it and stepped inside. Brian lingered outside.

Leland called him. "This old man needs to sit down. This is a bit much for me, Brian." He trudged to a chair at the kitchen table. "What are you doing out there?"

Brian entered with his eyes downcast and slumped onto a kitchen chair. Taking a deep breath, he studied the kitchen tabletop as he talked. "We have received a ransom note, directed to my wife, for a child named Grace Gilliver Richards. Sylvia was very upset, frantic really, so we called Sergeant Andrews." Brian was silent for a moment, then rueful. "Seems we've been seeing a lot of him lately."

"What else?" Leland asked, edging forward in his chair.

"A couple named Jericho reported their little girl's abduction one day before we got the ransom note, yesterday. Sylvia knows who they are. She had identified them through Ulrich as the original kidnappers–the ones who somehow rescued Grace from the train wreck that killed Lisa and little Jack. Or, possibly, she had been taken before then and that's one explanation for Lisa's crazy attempt to beat the train."

Now Leland stared at the table and rubbed his forehead. He felt his energy draining. "So, however those people got my granddaughter all those years ago, Ulrich saw a chance to make some money, and he's the one who has her now. Son-of-a-bitch."

"Except he doesn't," Brian said. "Sylvia told Andrews everything, and naturally they brought in the investigator. Turns out she'd been pushing for proof, something to test the child's DNA before confronting the Jericho's." Brian stood and paced to the kitchen window, his face turned away from Leland.

"The P.I. wanted to get something from the child and her so-called parents, but he was guilty of bad judgment when he hired a Russian couple, reliable if a bit unsavory, according to his sources. They must have done some investigation on their own and discovered Sylvia's trust fund."

"Then they saw an opportunity and expanded their job description to kidnapping?"

"Yes. Apparently Ulrich had nothing to do with that. So he says."

"Is that why you wanted the advance from me?" Leland asked. He had mixed two drinks from the still-stocked liquor cabinet and moved onto the screened porch overlooking the river. Even though his empty stomach lurched at the first sip, Brian's strange behavior caught his attention. The man could not sit still and would not look him in the eye.

"No. I mean, yes. In a manner of speaking, that is." Brian's mumbling only added to Leland's suspicion of him. "Not exactly. But, if Sylvia had not been taking money out of her trust fund for the P.I., she wouldn't have noticed my withdrawals. For business purposes."

"To cover up your spending habits?"

"No! I need to solve a thorny issue with a problem client."

"Well, yes, money does usually solve those thorny issues. I won't ask you for an accounting, Brian, especially considering our arrangement. But, all this stuff with Grace aside, I'm getting pretty damn tired of your excuses. You seem to forget how much money is at stake in our east side deal."

"Speaking of which." Brian sat down on the wicker settee then promptly stood again. He walked as he spoke. "I think your friend, Marsh Dalton, is behind legal contrivances to hide ownership of the property. But we can find no development plans. Here's something interesting though."

Brian began to wring his hands.

"For God's sake, what's wrong with you?" Leland asked.

"One of the old houses was bequeathed to a woman named Lorraine Jericho, who is now deceased, to be held in perpetuity for her heirs. This particular old house is held in an immutable land trust and cannot be sold."

"That's absurd. There's nothing that can't be bought if the money's right."

"The thing is," Brian paused and took a deep breath. "The man who owns it now is the man who kidnapped Grace, the first time, if she is, in fact, Grace. Charlie Jericho."

11

Dispatch

Sergeant Andrews trudged toward his office, his legs like leaden cannon balls. The dispatcher signaled to him, waving a fistful of pink phone message slips. He sighed.

"What's up, Sally?"

"It's Charlie Jericho again," she said, stuffing the wad of papers into his opened hand. "He keeps calling, wanting to find out if we know anything about his daughter. The last time he called, I think he was crying."

Andrews sighed again, thanked her and took the messages to his office. He shut the door and sat at his metal desk with his head in his hands. Slowly, he spread out the pink notes on top of his desk blotter. Sixteen. *This guy has all the red flags of a person of interest.* He glanced at a stack of files and picked up the top one. The Jericho' kidnapping case. *Something doesn't add up. Maybe he knows about the ransom demand to Sylvia Boggs. If he's in on it, he might be getting weak.*

Andrews reached for the phone to call his assistant to prepare a warrant, but it buzzed before he could pick it up. Sally's voice, "It's him again, Sergeant. What should I tell him?"

"Put him through." He punched a button and picked up the receiver. "Sergeant Andrews."

"Thank God I've got you, Sergeant. This is Charlie Jericho." The hoarse voice sounded strained.

As if I didn't know. "What can I do for you, Mr. Jericho?"

"Nothing except find my daughter. I'm so worried about her. I can't take it anymore. Don't you have any news?"

"Tell you what," Andrews said. "I'm on my way over to see you now." He hung up without waiting for Charlie's reply.

Fifteen minutes later, he pulled up to Charlie's house with another officer. A second car went to the alley behind it. Andrews doubted Charlie would run, but he took precautions. *Never know what these types might do.*

Charlie bounded down cement steps to the police car as Andrews got out. "What did you find? Do you know where she is?"

The officer with Andrews stepped forward and closed a handcuff around Charlie's left wrist. "Mr. Jericho," he said as he reached for Charlie's right arm. "You have the right to remain silent..."

Charlie's mouth flew open and he gaped at the officer as he wrenched his right arm away. "Oh, no! No you don't! I'm not who you should be arresting. This is just like the past. Someone does something wrong, even evil like this, and I'm there but I'm not involved. I get the blame–why? Why Sergeant Andrews? Because I'm poor or because I'm—"

120

He jerked away, howled and threw himself down on the ground, rolling and thrashing. But the officer and Andrews were instantly on top of him, pressing his face into the sparse stubble of grass that covered the front yard. Charlie screamed and kicked but finally settled into exhausted sobs and was subdued.

The officer finished reading Miranda rights and shoved Charlie into the back seat of the squad car. He sat with his head hung low, muttering. "What about my little girl? I don't understand. Why is this happening to me?"

Andrews went into the house. *Just a quick look around and I'll lock it for him.* He was surprised at the order and cleanliness. *There's love in this house.* He smelled fresh coffee and turned off the pot. Thoroughly but swiftly he checked every room. Then he locked the front door and pulled it shut.

Charlie gripped the arms of the chair tightly when they accused him of the abduction and kidnapping of Amy Jericho. He felt moisture welling up within his eyes, but he blinked hard to gain control of his emotions.

From a crisis-relief, untapped reservoir of strength, Charlie imagined his grandmother's face. Her words reverberated through him. "When you're down at the very bottom, child, remember to pray. The Lord will save you." *Why didn't I remember this until now?*

Silently and slowly, Charlie whispered a memorized Bible verse, also half-forgotten. *I will be with him in trouble. I will deliver him and honor him.* He took a deep breath and calmed himself. "I'm innocent," he said aloud to no one, "and the only thing that matters is finding Amy and putting my family together again."

He lifted his head, determined to act like a man instead of a victimized child.

Sylvia stood at the ornate cement railing of the veranda with a glass of chardonnay. Pewter clouds covered gathering dusk above the river valley. She settled that part of her senses expecting a ringing telephone. Police surveillance teams were in her living room with their listening and tracking equipment, but Brian was at an important meeting. *Those damn interminable meetings of his.*

She sipped wine and allowed herself to doubt. *What if this child isn't Grace? No! It must be. Why else would they make ransom demands to me? Her only living relative?*

"Well, her grandfather," she spoke aloud. "Curious that the kidnappers hadn't contacted Leland."

Sylvia shook her head and sipped again as the warmth of the wine spread within her. Smiling then, in spite of the circumstances, she allowed herself to make plans to bring Grace into her home–to raise the little girl as her own.

She was jolted from her dreamy reverie by shrill, cutting ringing. Her pulse jumped as she looked back to French doors that opened onto the veranda and saw the officer nod. With unsteady fingers, she pressed talk on the cordless phone she held.

"Hello."

"Missus Boggs." The man's voice was thick with malice and an unfamiliar, heavy accent. "You got money?"

"Who are you? Where's Grace? Is she okay?" Sylvia choked on her own anxiety. She could not breathe.

A menacing laugh. "So many questions, Missus Boggs."

The police technician motioned for Sylvia to keep talking, but her throat froze. She swallowed hard. "Where are you?"

"No questions. She okay now. You bring money, alone, tonight or she not okay. No money, no girl."

Sylvia gasped. "Where? What do you want me to do?"

"Later." The man hung up.

Sylvia's stricken eyes found the officer, shaking his head. The half-full wine glass slipped from her fingers, crashing onto the cement floor, shattering into pieces.

It was nearly 10:00 p.m. Sylvia was jumpy as a cat in a thunderstorm. Brian had come home at last with the money, but he was no comfort to her. He paced and fidgeted. His obvious anxiety only annoyed her.

Sergeant Andrews had also arrived, grim-faced and serious. "The tracking device," he explained, "is concealed within one of the bound stacks of money. Another one is in the lining of the gym bag containing it, but kidnappers often know that so they discard the bag as soon as possible."

Sylvia was dressed in loose black slacks, a black sweater and soft-soled black running shoes. Her role was to follow the kidnapper's directions; undercover police would follow her.

Brian protested sending her alone, but Sylvia insisted. "I can do this, Brian," she said, even as her stomach fluttered. "Sergeant Andrews said they only want money. I only want Grace."

Brian retreated to a corner chair, glum and resigned.

At exactly 10:15 p.m. the phone rang. Sylvia picked it up but didn't speak. The same voice, this time in a whisper, said, "Listen,

Missus Boggs. Old meat packing plant. Railroad yard. Bring money, alone, or no child. Be there eleven." He hung up.

Sophisticated tracking equipment set up in Sylvia's living room had traced the first call to a throw-away cell phone, dashing Sylvia's hopes of finding Grace before the ransom drop. She pretended courage and prayed Grace was not hurt.

At 10:30 p.m. she left in her Lexus with the gym bag. Driving slowly, she wound through quiet residential streets surrounding her house heading east. She took deep breaths though her heart hammered, and she stifled a sob as she drove over the railroad crossing. *Where this all began.* She passed the small cluster of houses on Sparrow Street aware Charlie Jericho lived in one of them. Her anger flared.

At the deserted plant, there was a broken lock on big chain-link gates. One side had been forced open wide enough to allow a car to slide through. Swallowing hard, she eased the Lexus in-between the gates into the parking lot. It was a clear autumn night and moonlight flooded the deserted lot.

She pulled around the plant to hide from the road, though she doubted her own judgment. She turned off the car engine and waited. It was 10:50 p.m. She was early.

In shadows cast by the huge building, she imagined movement. She strained her eyes to make it out, but there was nothing. She pressed her heels down hard to stop her legs from shaking. Then, again, movement more black than the darkness surrounding it.

She leaned forward and turned on the car's auxiliary power to lower her window. Autumn chill combined with nerves and she shivered.

A shape came into view, a large man walking toward her. Ten feet in front of the car he stopped and motioned for her to come to him.

With trembling knees, she stepped out, gym bag in hand. Sylvia memorized his features–dark, bushy hair, a full beard, and huge shoulders.

Like a robot, she glided toward him. Eight feet, six feet, four feet–

Suddenly, a woman screamed. The man grabbed Sylvia's hair and pulled her toward him. She yelped and dropped the gym bag. He put his other arm around her neck and drug her back into the shadows. She panicked, choking and flailing like a trapped mongrel in his arms.

In the dim cover, he released his hold on her neck and struck her hard across the face. "I say alone. Now you pay more. No child." His voice growled.

He shoved her into gravel and kicked her ribs. She gasped and cried out. He sprinted to the gym bag, clearly visible in the moonlit parking lot. With one deft move, he scooped it up, pivoted and ran back toward Sylvia.

Then, a piercing blast made the man twist in mid-stride, stumble and right himself. Two more steps, nearly upon her now, and Sylvia shuddered at another thunderous blast, closer and louder still.

He tripped to his knees, reaching out for her. She couldn't move, squeezed her eyes shut and gagged. An earth-shaking thud reverberated through her when the man fell forward, his face only inches from hers. She registered his pockmarked face, a blank look in his open eyes. His gaping mouth revealing stained, yellowed teeth. The foul stench of his feces assaulted her. Inching back from the horror, she vomited and lost consciousness.

Andrews' face came into focus. He shook her shoulder, spoke her name. A searing pain ripped through her side when she moved and her jaw pounded with sharp throbs. Andrews and another officer helped her to her feet and half-carried her to the loading dock. She sat, back propped against a stack of old pallets. They gave her water to drink.

Each sip was painful but she attained an aching awareness of where she was and what had happened.

Sylvia answered their questions slowly. Yes, she was all right. Sort of. They were going to drive her to the hospital. They had good news.

She let herself be led past the spot where the man fell, covered now with a blanket. Shaking, raw and fragile, she slid into the squad car's back seat.

"It's been three days since my little girl went missing." Mae sagged against the door frame of the hospital administrator's office. Her chin trembled and she pushed back her tangled brown hair with a careless thrust.

For a moment, the administrator peered at her over the top of the glasses he wore perpetually perched on the bridge of his nose. Then, he hopped up and hurried around his desk to pull out a chair for her.

"Mae, please sit down."

Mae crumpled into the chair while he leaned into the hallway, checking both ways before shutting the door.

Taking her small cold hand into both of his warm ones, he said, "My dear, I'm so sorry for what you're going through. Everyone here at Mercy is."

His gentle voice had a soothing effect on Mae, and her ragged breathing began to calm. He had peppermint on his breath. The administrator settled himself behind his desk again.

"You wanted to see me," Mae said. "Flora told me when I called in, but you can see I'm in no condition to work." She chewed on her lower lip and couldn't figure out what to do with her hands.

"Yes, yes. You know we've always valued your work here, Mae."

"Am I going to be fired?" Mae fought to keep panic out of her voice. She squeezed the arms of her chair to steady herself.

"No, no," he said. "This is a bit of a delicate matter." He cleared his throat. "I think you should take a leave of absence until she is found."

"So I'm not fired?" Mae felt weak with relief. "But I can go home now?"

"Yes, but I must ask you to turn in your badge. For the time being."

"I don't understand. If I'm not being fired, why do I have to turn in my badge?"

The administrator looked uncomfortable, and Mae worried without knowing exactly why. *He's hiding something from me. God, don't let it be more bad news.*

"I had hoped to give you good news today, but it's a complicated situation."

Mae waited, swallowing a cold fist of fear that threatened to choke her.

"What do you mean?"

"There was a little girl brought in last night—"

Mae jumped to her feet. "Is it my Amy? I want to see her!"

"I'm afraid that's impossible, dear. You see, we believe we know who she is." He lifted the corner of a file folder on his desk and peered inside. He searched her face before he said, "She's Grace Gilliver Richards."

Mae bolted from the office and ran through the hallway, oblivious of everyone and everything. *Amy! Oh my baby, you're alive!* She ran up the stairs two at a time until she got to the pediatric floor, her floor.

At the nurse's station, Crystal and the head nurse, Flora, were shocked when she ran past. Crystal called to her, but then turned to answer a ringing telephone. *First to the ward. No, no, they'd put her in a private room.*

At the end of the hallway, a uniformed policeman was leaning against the wall outside of a room. *That must be where she is.* Mae slowed to a brisk walk, smoothed her clothes with her hands and smiled. As she reached the room, the officer's cell phone rang. Behind her Crystal and Flora were charging toward her. She took a deep breath, gulped and pushed past the guard into the room.

Mae shrieked when she saw Amy sitting on the bed. The girl looked up, grinned, bounded from the bed and ran toward her. "Mommy! Mommy!"

"Amy!"

In an instant, the police officer grasped Mae's upper arms from behind and pulled her, struggling, through the door. The nurses rushed in to grab Amy and hold her in the room.

Outside the door, Mae was handcuffed and led away, screaming. "You don't understand! You have to let me go! That's my daughter!"

"Orders, ma'am," the officer barked. He held her firmly. The last sound before he thrust her into an empty elevator was Amy's terror-stricken voice.

"MOMMY! MOMEEEE!"

"Listen, you prick," Marsh Dalton hissed into the telephone. "I pay big bucks to your hot shot Washington firm to keep my business private.

How dare you tell me my privacy's been compromised? What the hell does that mean anyway?"

He paused for explanation, then exploded into the receiver again. "I don't care how you do it, but you goddamn better get it done. And I mean now." He crushed the receiver into its cradle.

Incredulous, he stared at the phone. He hurried behind his desk and unlocked the drawer with the false bottom. Relieved after a quick examination, he shut it and composed himself. Nothing was there to tie his name to the trust documents, or worse.

He went to his private washroom, splashed citrus-scented water on his face to tighten his pores and stared into the mirror. *Eikens. Thomas Eikens must be behind this. Well, I'll have to see about that.*

Marsh Dalton combed his smooth, silver hair, put on his suit coat and straightened his tie. Slamming the door a bit too hard, he left his office, thinking to have a quiet lunch and finish reading his daily newspapers. He had devoured the *Wall Street Journal* and the *New York Times* in the morning, as was his habit. Afternoons he saved for local news and lighter, fluffier stuff, *The Tillman Tattler*.

Seated at a corner table at the club, he picked at a large Cobb salad with meticulous care, then settled back with his coffee to read the paper. It was filled with the usual articles about local low-life's and civic activities. Nothing interested him until he glanced over the police blotter, and a small notice leapt out.

POLICE:

Suspicion of kidnapping, Charlie Jericho, 1211 Sparrow St.

Small hairs on the back of his neck bristled. *What the hell? This is all I need.* The words went in and out of focus for several seconds. He folded the paper and sat back to lose himself out the window in the lush fall foliage surrounding Tillman's Country Club. He allowed his mind to drift like the yellow and red leaves floating down in the breeze.

Rachel, damn. I miss her even now. My only son ended up being raised in that same dumpy house.

Marsh closed his eyes and rubbed his forehead. It wouldn't do to have people find out. Good thing that secret trust, buried under layers of legal nuances for the aging grandmother and the boy, was untraceable. Should his enemies try. Until now. *Damn.*

When he opened his eyes, he saw Leland Richards and that irritating lawyer, Brian Boggs, watching him. They gestured amiably, and Marsh nodded but didn't stop to greet them as he left.

Driving away though, he had a sudden flash of insight. *They're the ones behind my exposure. Why didn't I see it? Damn.* He slapped the steering wheel of his Cadillac with the palm of his hand.

Familiar warmth flooded his face, his chest, and finally his arms and legs. Anger always made him feel warm and this time it was fed by resentment. He began to formulate his plans. *Might be time to feed the fuel of Eikens' fury again. As long as he believes his harassment is coming from Leland, he'll keep Leland too busy to pursue me.*

12

Repercussions

The shelter care hearing for the child was held first thing the next morning, when the girl was still in the hospital. The juvenile Court judge appointed a *guardian ad litem* to work with DCFS to establish temporary custody. The judge considered these hearings routine, but even he was intrigued by the circumstances of the kidnapping and rescue.

Sergeant Andrews had notified the State's attorney after his meeting with Crystal Winston. Both men agreed. The unusual ransom demand and Sylvia Boggs' allegations together with the new information from Crystal Winston gave them enough to consider charges against Charlie and Mae Jericho. When they filled in the juvenile court judge, he granted Sylvia Boggs' request to attend the hearing. He listened raptly to her story.

"Your honor," she said. "I hardly know where to begin. My sister, as you probably know, was killed in a train wreck along with my nephew nearly seven years ago. Her daughter, my niece, was only two months old at the time, and her body was never found."

Sylvia winced but kept speaking. "I believe this little girl who was rescued last night is my niece. I also think she was taken from the accident scene, or possibly shortly before the accident, by a man named Charlie Jericho and kept as his own, along with his wife, for all of these years."

The judge nodded.

"In fact, I'm sure of it," Sylvia said.

At this the judge raised his eyebrows. "How can you be so sure, Mrs. Boggs? Have you ever seen the child?"

"Yes sir. Three times and she's my sister's daughter. I'd swear to it."

"What proof do you have?"

"None except my own memory and the way she looked exactly like my sister did at her age."

The judge leaned back in his chair, smiled indulgently. "Now surely you can't expect the Court to take any kind of custody action based upon how a child looks," he said. "Of course, there is the unusual situation of the ransom being demanded of you, and your husband, I believe."

"Absolutely," Sylvia said. "Why would they come to us for money unless they knew? This child is a member of our family."

The judge shuffled some papers in front of him. "It's my understanding that she is the alleged granddaughter of Leland Richards of GillRich Construction too. Why didn't they contact him, do you think?"

"You'd have to ask them, except–except…" Sylvia fumbled in her pocket for a tissue, but Brian handed her a monogrammed handkerchief.

"Your honor," Brian said. "I think it's ridiculous you're questioning my wife. She's just witnessed the murder of a criminal, and this whole thing has been quite upsetting to her."

"I didn't give you permission to speak, counselor," the judge said. "Why would I not believe the family who's cared for her for, what is it—six or seven years—isn't her biological family?"

"Because I told you," Sylvia raised her voice. "I'm a Gilliver; my family's been leaders in this community for years."

The judge spoke louder. "I'm aware of who your father was, Mrs. Boggs. However, I see no bearing on this case. Is there anything, anything at all, that would provide a positive identification of this minor?"

Sylvia didn't reply.

"Mrs. Boggs, do you know a woman by the name of Crystal Winston?"

Sylvia thought for a moment. "No sir."

"At this time," he shuffled more papers, "I'm appointing Jonathan Lee as the minor's *guardian ad litem* and attorney. The Department of Child and Family Services will take the matter to the State's attorney's lawyer regarding custody if their investigation warrants it."

Sylvia glared at him.

The judge glared back. "However," he said. "It is within my jurisdiction and judgment to issue an order for genetic testing. You will be notified of any further Court actions."

"Thank you, your honor," Sylvia said. Her most nourished belief was about to be realized.

"Mr. Jericho," the detective's voice was cool. "Where is your daughter now?"

Charlie fixed him with a wary gaze. "I wish I knew. Then this whole thing would be over. You should be finding her, not asking me questions I've already answered." Charlie sat straighter in his chair, looking brighter and more alert. "Amy needs me. Somehow, someway, we'll find her, and the truth will come out. I love that little girl."

"You told us someone had taken you and her away in a van. What happened then?"

"I couldn't save her. They tied me up and hurt me. Oh, God." He glared at the detective.

"They're not going to hurt her, are they? Oh God. Why are you wasting so much time? We should all be looking for her."

Stepping out of the stark interrogation room, the detective conferred with Sergeant Andrews. "I'm not sure," he said. "His story is consistent and he might be one of those sensitive guys who fall apart when something like this happens. I think he's telling the truth."

"Yes," said Andrews. "I can't help feeling sorry for the guy. He doesn't know we have his wife in custody or that we've rescued a little girl who Sylvia Boggs claims is her niece, not his daughter. We need some evidence or a worthwhile lead to untangle this whole mess. He may not have anything to do with this abduction, but something is definitely wrong here."

"Okay. I'll try again in a few minutes. Let him cool down first. One thing though," the detective said. "The scars on his face look strange. The angle makes it look like he did them himself."

"In cases like this, the aftermath can be too great to bear. He may have faked all his injuries."

The interminable interrogation continued. Charlie was finally taken to a cell where he sat calmly staring at the wall, looking dejected, but mentally fishing in the deep well of his long neglected faith for hope.

He was charged with suspicion of kidnapping. Bond was set at $10,000 while the department scurried to put together the pieces of the Amy Jericho-Grace Gilliver Richards case. A blood sample from the child was being evaluated.

One day later Charlie was released. A donor anonymous to him paid his bail.

Mae had never been charged.

Jimmy Noble wanted to comfort his wife but he didn't know how. Nora sat next to him, crying.

"Those poor people," she said. "I can't even begin to imagine what they're going through. Why, I've never seen a child as bright and happy as Amy. She's obviously well-cared for and well-loved."

"Uh huh," Jimmy whispered. He lifted his hand to pat Nora in what he hoped was a gentle, consoling gesture, but he couldn't do it. Truth was he had little sympathy for Charlie Jericho based on their history. *The man damn near killed me out of ignorance. What kind of a father would he make?*

Still, Jimmy reflected on the good days too, before the wood shop accident that nearly took his life. He shook his head as if to deny the truth about Charlie. Kind-hearted, well-intentioned Charlie. Long ago, he could have taken such a different path.

"Well, maybe," he said, wrapping his arms around Nora and pulling her close. "Charlie got mixed up in something he couldn't handle and his little girl is collateral damage. Did you ever think of that?"

Nora pushed away from him. "I don't know what you mean." She wiped the tears from her cheeks with the back of her hand. "He walks her to and from school every day, hand in hand. She adores him and he loves her. You can see it in his face. Amy is—was—cherished." She choked on the words.

"You are getting too attached to people you don't know, Nora," Jimmy said. His thoughts were clouded again with memories of the accident. "Charlie Jericho is an easy victim for the wrong kind of people. He might not mean to hurt his daughter, but he can't protect her either."

Nora's expression was full of questions, but she didn't speak. Jimmy went on.

"There's a certain element, even here in Tillman, which preys upon weaknesses and misfortunes of others." He took Nora's hand. "A person needs to be alert, and Charlie sure isn't that. No one would kidnap that child with intent of getting a ransom out of Charlie. He has no money."

Jimmy paused to rub his chin, looking absently across the room. "My guess is that a pedophile is involved, especially since you say Amy is so precocious, so bright and attractive."

"Oh my God. No." Nora's tears now spilled over her cheeks.

He frowned and searched his mind for a scrap of memory that eluded him. There was something he could not quite recall tugging at his thoughts. *Or maybe…*

Nora dried her eyes with a tissue and straightened her shoulders. "You have to help find her. You're good at helping people, Jimmy."

"Sure." Jimmy's thoughts were still preoccupied with something he could not quite grasp, but then he had a flash of insight.

Sanders.

Tillman, Tennessee, is becoming a place of miserable people. Sergeant Andrews reflected as he sipped his morning coffee. *Must keep an eye on the Jericho's—Charlie and Mae— something's wrong there. Dysfunctional? Criminal? Certainly Crystal Winston thinks so.*

He strode with purpose from his office toward the jail infirmary.

After the bungled ransom pick up, the woman had become hysterical, lashing out at officers who took her into custody. She'd smashed a cell phone against one officer's skull with surprising strength. Then, she'd kicked another's groin, bringing him to his knees. Her near escape ended when a third officer tackled her to the floor.

In the squad car, she had screamed incessantly in an unintelligible language. She'd scratched, kicked and bit at every chance until finally, still thrashing and shouting she was injected with Haldol by Dr. Simon.

One shot was not enough. She had turned from attacking her captors to self-inflicted violence. Deep, bloody gouges raked across her face and arms.

Dr. Simon was waiting for him. "She's quiet now," he said as Andrews peered through a small glass window into the stark cell. "We cut her fingernails before we put her into a straightjacket, but she's stable now. You can question her if you can get someone to speak her language."

"Thanks, doc. The FBI is sending an interpreter today along with a team of investigators. It'll be their case now." Andrews sighed with relief.

The FBI arrived mid-morning and spent an hour going over the facts of the case before they interrogated the woman.

An hour after that, Fenn, the lead investigator, stepped into Andrews' office without knocking and shut the door. He was a grim-faced man in an impeccable navy-blue suit, groomed to look as non-descript as possible.

"You've stumbled onto something here, Andrews," he said. "Who would've thought these people would surface in a place like Tillman?" He jerked a chair to the front of the desk, sat down and leaned forward. "We've been trying to crack a white-slavery ring that's been operating in big cities across the south for months now."

That got Andrews' attention. "White slavery? No, no, this is a kidnapping case."

"That's how they all begin. Most victims are smuggled out of the country. I suspect this woman is one of the leaders of the Russian ring responsible for seven abductions this year alone. Her name is Elena Volskaya."

"What about the man? And the ransom attempt?"

"We think he was her husband. They were part of a group of Russian aliens who've been operating most recently in the Birmingham area. It's a stroke of luck for us that you nailed her–she might lead us to the rest. We may even be able to find some victims and bring down other groups involved in the same scheme." He cleared his throat. "As for the ransom, that's usually not their MO, but they must have learned this particular child had a rich family. So, they branched out."

Andrews studied papers on top of his desk for a moment. "Well, as you know from the file, there's quite a story with this little girl."

Fenn nodded.

"We now have DNA test results proving she's related to the Gilliver family. And, if she's the child thought to have perished in a train wreck seven years ago, as Sylvia Gilliver Boggs claims," Andrews paused. "She's not related to her deceased mother's husband."

"These things happen," Fenn put the fingers of his hand together in a tent-like gesture and frowned at them. "Perhaps she had an extra-marital affair and the child's the result. I'm intrigued by the story with the Jericho couple. How did they get her and how were they able to keep up the act for so many years? They don't seem very sophisticated."

"They're not," Andrews said. "In fact, Charlie Jericho is some-what limited. At first, we thought he had something to do with the kidnapping, for ransom money. His version of the crime seemed unbe-lievable, and his injuries were suspicious, perhaps self-inflicted. The little girl's birth certificate is from a hospital over near Cartersville for a live birth to a Pat Walker, Mae Jericho's sister. Funny thing though, the hospital has no record of the birth, and we can't locate Pat Walker."

"We can have our document experts check it. The girl is clearly not who they say she is." Fenn stood and pushed his chair back. "Now that it's our case, we'll bring them in for questioning again."

Brian drummed his fingertips on the empty top of his ornate desk while resting his chin on his other hand. His thoughts swam from one problem to another.

He had learned Marsh Dalton owned the east side parcel Leland wanted to divert to his own use and profit. But Leland didn't know

Brian planned a touch of blackmail. Marsh had something to hide, and Brian had found out what it was.

Charlie Jericho's birth records were not filed with the county. That was common with home births, especially among the poor. Following a hunch, he'd managed to uncover some old, archived hospital records. Poor Charlie had several health problems as an infant. At one point, doctors had recommended him for a children's institution one hundred miles away.

Most useful were two old records showing his parents as Rachel Jericho and Marshall Charles Dalton. Brian relished the possibilities. All public records for Charlie or for Rachel Jericho had then disappeared until the will of one Lorraine Jericho ceded the deed for her modest house to Charlie D. Jericho.

Here Brian paused in his scheming to wonder about Rachel. He hadn't been able to locate a death certificate. Suicide?

He smiled to himself. Yes, Marsh would surely pay to keep that information private. Once paid, Brian would reveal it anyway, to Leland. Of course, Marsh wouldn't know who was behind his fall. Brian planned to use certain individuals.

With Leland, Brian had contrived a carefully constructed straw company, which included sham contracts for consulting fees to draft development plans for the river corridor. In reality, funds from private investors and government would flow directly into their pockets. A sufficiently unsuspicious portion would find its way into GillRich's west side development.

When the bogus company declared bankruptcy, with ironclad fraudulent figures, Leland and GillRich would sweep in to develop the east side, with more investors and government money. The only thing that remained to put the plan into action was for Leland to acquire the property, secretly and cheaply.

Brian stood and stretched, smiling. He was well on his way to becoming an independently wealthy man. The annoying buzz of his phone startled him out of his reverie.

"That's great, Sylvia," he said. "Uh huh. That soon? Listen, are you sure that's what you really want? What if it turns out the girl is not Grace, after all?"

He paused to listen for a long moment. "No, nothing's wrong. I'm preoccupied with work, that's all. And, I'm a little surprised DCFS will get test results so soon."

He blinked several times with a touch of irritation while she replied. "Got to get back to work now, darling. I'll see you tonight."

After hanging up, he crossed the room to pour a scotch, inhaled its sharp tang and then stood staring out the window.

The problem is Grace. Sylvia was determined to adopt her, and Brian couldn't allow anyone to know about his connection to Grace. It could spoil everything, with Sylvia and even with Leland.

As he mused over ugly possibilities, he kept coming back to only one conclusion.

No one must find out about Grace. At any cost.

Charlie felt defeated, but Mae seemed buoyed, almost cheerful, after their interrogation by the FBI.

"Good thing we didn't tell them we learned who Amy really was, back then," she said. Her fair eyes danced. "We're innocent victims, Good Samaritans."

Charlie stared at her, open-mouthed, but kept silent.

"It's such good news they let us come home, Charlie, and she's going to be taken to a temporary foster home, at least until Sylvia Boggs gets involved."

Charlie's head began to throb. "Good news?"

"Yes!" Mae sat next to him and took his cold hand into her two warm ones.

"Why?" His hope flickered. Maybe *Mae does really still love me.*

"Don't you see, Charlie? We know she's okay, first of all, but we also know where she is."

"I don't get it, Mae. We've lost Amy."

Mae smiled at him.

Must be the first time in days.

"We're still her parents." Mae's blue eyes transformed to deep, wet pools. "Poor thing. She's been through so much."

Charlie put his other hand over hers. "But Mae—"

"We have to go get her. I'm sure she'd rather be with us. We can be ready to leave. I don't care about the house or money. You're a great carpenter, Charlie, and I'm an experienced nurse's aide. We'll find work, someplace far away, and start over. You, me and Amy."

He pulled his hands away. "Mae, it's not right."

"Oh, don't be crazy. Of course it's right. Amy belongs with us. She's our gift from God."

Mae snuggled against Charlie, then stood and took a folded piece of paper and a stubby pencil from her pocket. "Now all we need is a plan."

Charlie felt a constricting sensation in his gut and bolted to the bathroom.

Late at night, Marsh listened intently to a garbled voice on the phone. Since no one was at his office, he pressed the speaker button so he could pace, in a vain attempt to calm himself.

When the caller had finished his accusations, Marsh bellowed, "Who the hell is this?"

The voice laughed. "You'll never know, Dalton. But there's a way you can keep it out of the newspaper." Another laugh.

"Well, money, of course. But listen you, who do you think you are? You can't prove anything."

"Don't have to," the loud, impersonal voice said. "There's enough the local newspaper will print it anyway."

"That rag! Nobody will believe it."

"If you want to take that chance, we're—"

"We! What do you mean we? Who the hell are you?" Marsh was aware of his heart thumping in his chest and perspiration seeping through his clothes.

The audacious laugh again. "As I was saying, Dalton, if you want to play games, that little tidbit is only the beginning. We have more."

Marsh panicked. "More? What? You scumbag. You can't bully me!"

"Think about it. For the right amount of money you can make it all go away, Daddy."

The caller hung up leaving Marsh frayed and bruised inside. His own sweat reeked of fear and it disgusted him. *No. It can't be. No one can know about that.*

Marsh strolled along corridors of the old museum, stopping to feign interest in several exhibits. It was nearly closing time, and his hand twitched on the handle of the executive briefcase he carried. No one seemed to notice his presence or behavior.

After all, I'm on the museum board as well as on the board of the construction firm building the addition. I should be able to stay as long as I like. Wish to hell that SOB would hurry though.

As Marsh turned into a deserted gallery of ancient Native American artifacts, he heard a noise behind him from a shadowy corner. In an instant he felt cold metal against the back of his head and froze.

"Don't turn around, Dalton." The voice was muffled and disguised through some kind of a device. Like a voice box.

"Set the briefcase down."

Marsh swallowed hard. "The documents?"

The gun clicked. *Oh my God. This idiot's going to kill me!* Marsh dropped the briefcase.

In one swift movement, the phantom behind the words grabbed the briefcase and pushed Marsh forward sprawling on the unyielding tile floor. By the time Marsh caught his breath and struggled to his feet, the man was gone.

There in the middle of the tiles lay a manila envelope. Marsh snatched it up and looked around. No one in sight. He ripped open the end of the bulky envelope and yanked out a sheaf of papers. His panic and rage surged as he rifled through the pages, front and back.

Every single page was blank.

13

Legal Action

Sergeant Andrews wasn't sure who leaked the story to the press, but he gave up trying to find fault. He did his best to thwart the media interest in Charlie and Mae's case. It was no use. In the small town of Tillman, Tennessee, this was the biggest story since he couldn't remember when.

Interviews of the local prosecutor, Ryan H.B. Evans, were in every edition of every newspaper across the State as well as on statewide TV news broadcasts. A tall, thin man with hawkish features and eyes the color of pitch, Evans projected the confident assurance of someone who felt undisputedly right. Standing on the steps of the county courthouse in bald sunlight, he portrayed modesty with outstretched hands.

"Folks, folks, now nothing's been tried yet, but the way I see it..."

"Mr. Evans, will you ask for jail time? What's going to happen to the little girl now? Were they in on the kidnapping?"

The reporters clustered around him with outstretched microphones.

"It's up to the Court to decide," he said, "but the way I see it they knew they were doing something wrong. They are guilty of a first kidnapping if not the second one."

The charges against Mae and Charlie differed, but only slightly. Mae was also charged with falsifying records, a forgery charge. Both of them had given remarkably consistent stories. "Because that's the truth," Charlie's Court-appointed defender, Jed Hamilton, said. Together with Mae's attorney, Alex Nathan Noonis, who insisted everyone call him Nate, they had successfully moved to drop the charge of aggravated kidnapping to a lesser kidnapping charge, one that would carry a lighter penalty. It was clear that Amy or Grace had not been confined against her will. Both young public defenders were passionate, if inexperienced, and were buoyed at this small success. The police investigation into her recent abduction had exonerated Charlie and Mae of any involvement in that ugliness, though Evans still hinted at their involvement.

In the weeks following their indictment, the number of interviews had gotten way out of hand, to Andrews' way of thinking. The public outcry was fed by irresponsible or at least questionable statements by Evans that were exploited by the press. It became clear the prosecutor's objective was to make Charlie and Mae objects of such despicable character that no one could find them innocent. He hinted several times of mental imbalances and wayward intentions. The public might deduce their treatment of little Amy had been abusive or fraught with unhealthy implications.

Andrews watched Sylvia Boggs closely from the sidelines. She had a family connection to the prosecutor, Ryan H.B. Evans. *Heck, who in power didn't she have a connection to?* True to her upper class breeding, Sylvia refrained from public comment and wore a mask of sterile emotion in front of the cameras. Still, Andrews wondered about her motive. *Did she want extreme punishment for the Jericho's?*

There had been a similar case years ago in another part of the state in which an infant was abducted and brought up as the child of the offender. Then, it turned out the infant's real parents didn't want him and had in fact tried to sell the child to a couple. Appalled, the couple saw it as poetic justice to take the child away and disappear. Even though they were discovered years later, they had no remorse. The boy had grown strong and smart and was on his high school football team, which made all-state. That was their fatal mistake. When his photo appeared with the winning team, his biological parents started asking questions. He'd had the misfortune to look exactly like his father had at that age. They sought huge sums of money for their damages and tore apart an apparently happy and well-adjusted family life. The case had ended badly for the boy who went into foster care in another part of the state.

Statements to the press by the defense for both Charlie and Mae were short and simple. "They did nothing wrong. They raised the child with all the love anyone could give."

"You know Charlie has a record, don't you?" Prosecutor Evans told the judge in chambers.

"That has no bearing here," Jed Hamilton said. The young attorney's straight brown hair stuck up in a cowlick on top, and he smoothed it down as he planted his feet a bit farther apart and stood a bit straighter.

"On the contrary," Evans gave a condescending snort. "It shows the character of the defendant, and I think the jury has a right to know what kind of people they are."

"He was a teenager and got involved with some rough guys—"

"Other low-life's like him from that skuzzy area by the tracks, no doubt." Evans barely concealed his sneer.

Hamilton ignored the interruption. "He had taken a ride from them and happened to be in the car when they stopped to rob a gas station. He was remanded to his grandmother's custody, and she made sure he didn't get in trouble again."

Evans waived his hand in dismissal. "It shows a lack of judgment on his part, but we can dispense with the jury trial. The case is so clear; a bench trial is all that's needed."

"Your honor," Hamilton addressed the judge. "My client does not waive his rights to a jury trial."

"Mine either," Noonis said.

"I'm amazed at you gentlemen." Evans pretended distress. "If you put your clients in front of a jury on the witness stand, I'll eat them alive." He relished the idea.

"They are innocent," Hamilton said, "of any premeditated wrongdoing and I intend to prove it."

"You can't tell me the forgery was unintentional."

Noonis answered Evans this time. "That applies only to my client, Mae Jericho, and there was no malicious intent to defraud. I intend to show simple negligence."

"Hah!" Evans laughed. Standing, he crossed his arms over his chest and glared down at both of the younger attorneys. "I suggest you check the statutes for each of these charges. Plus, public opinion clearly favors the little girl's welfare."

"Gentlemen," the judge said. "I'm the one who interprets penal code. Mr. Evans, these defendants want their cases brought before their peers, so at this time, I'm setting it for the earliest available date on my docket. Get your cases in order, counselors."

"But Judge," Hamilton protested. "We need time to prepare—"

"Nonsense. I agree with Prosecutor Evans, though I admit that's rare. You public defenders want the trial to be as far away from the incident as possible. But in this situation, from what I know, time isn't on the side of your clients or in their best interests."

Evans smiled but didn't speak.

The judge stood, effectively dismissing all three attorneys.

Charlie and Mae were catapulted to local infamy overnight. Like captives in their own home, they were being watched. When they did venture out, always together for comfort and support, they endured stares, whispers and bold scorn.

Mae wandered from Charlie's side at the grocery store to go back to the pasta aisle. A grey-haired woman gaped at her. She backed away from Mae until she bumped into her husband who led her away by the elbow hissing over his shoulder at Mae, "You should be ashamed." Mae dropped the package of noodles and fled back to Charlie, her eyes squinted and bleak.

"What happened?" Charlie asked.

Mae snapped her head back and forth and pressed her lips together, eyes straight ahead. Charlie pushed the cart a bit faster.

Not everyone was hostile to them though. At the checkout counter, old Mercer passed a note to Charlie and whispered. "Here's the number of a woman who wants some cabinets repaired. It's a small job but she's heard of your work and asked me about you. She's okay with hiring you."

Charlie stuffed the note into his pocket without looking at it. "Thank you. We could sure use the money."

Negative publicity and liability exposure fears had forced Mercy Hospital's board to let Mae go. After all, the feeling was, she worked with children. But the administrator phoned a few weeks later.

"This is strictly off the record, dear. You're going through a hard time. A family came to me looking for a nurse to come in to care for an elderly man during the day. They can't pay too much, but they are willing to hire you. If you're interested, of course."

So Mae went discreetly to work in a private residence, and Charlie found a few projects to help keep them going. The quiet of their house without Amy fell around them like a prison sentence they both feared and, sometimes, welcomed.

"I'm beginning to see," Charlie said. His tawny face was smooth as the cloudless amber sunset Mae could see behind his shoulder. "We were supposed to have a place in Amy's life, not to be her life."

Mae frowned. This husband of hers was becoming more mysterious to her day by day. "What do you mean?" She settled next to him in their tiny backyard, inhaling the scent of fresh mown grass.

"Well, we have been so lucky, Mae."

"Lucky?"

"Yes, to have had Amy at all. They're about to punish us for keeping her." Here Charlie paused, searching for the right words. "But whatever they do to us, they can't take away the good years, the good times, the good memories."

Mae sighed and leaned into Charlie, feeling his firm strength as a solid comfort. *Is he saying it's not about us? But what about the pain?*

Charlie continued. "We taught her all about love, as much as we could show. So, she will always know what that feels like—what being loved is—like I know I was loved by Nana."

Mae wanted to jump up and shout, "No! That's not right! She's ours!" But her heart told her Charlie was right, and in silence she let his peace and his warmth wash over her. A sad nostalgia drifted around them as they sat in the dusk, holding each other now. Even though affection had been absent in her childhood, Mae connected with his words.

Mae reveled in Charlie's love for her.

Evans blanketed the Court with motions and the young defenders fired blindly back, creating a paper war that extended each deadline by weeks. The grinding process of the legal system exaggerated the timeline.

Eventually, though, the final continuances were exhausted, and the trial date loomed. Charlie's attorney, Jed Hamilton, didn't want to cut a deal with Evans, or even with Mae's attorney, "Nate" Noonis, because he could throw the case on the mercy of the Court, after presenting Charlie's good qualities, of course.

Noonis, however, was looking for damage control. He knew Mae to be the more culpable of the two because of the falsification of records, and also her mere literacy could be seen to make Charlie look like a victim. Evans shrugged off suggestions for plea bargains, show-ing disinterest or pointing out the strengths of his case but never quite closing the door all the way. So, Noonis, with nothing but pity and sympathy for his client, set about amassing a list of positive character references. He could present her as a good person, who'd made a mis-take, albeit compounded, but had only good intent.

Charlie and Mae sat at separate tables in the courtroom with their separate attorneys. Charlie's face above his neat beard was pinched and drained, emphasizing his cheekbones and a certain vulnerability. His calm demeanor, though, exuded a much understated strength that made people trust him.

Mae was a contrast. Her eyes were watering, and she communi-cated her embarrassment and fear. Nate, her kind but serious attorney, warned her to relax. Weak-kneed, she wobbled when the judge entered the courtroom and willed herself to breathe deeply. Everything she tried to calm herself didn't work.

But when they all were seated again, the judge smiled at her. Probably Charlie too, but she didn't turn around.

If this is what she had to go through to maybe get Amy back, she most certainly would get herself under control. If she could.

It had been nearly a year since she'd seen Amy. Mae let her mind lapse into the memory of her last morning with Amy. *If only I'd known.* The lawyers were making their opening statements. Mae snuck a glance at Charlie who sat attentive, interested. How she'd loved him when she'd carried his child. She'd loved him like words caressing the printed pages he so wanted to read.

The trial lasted three full days. Evans presented his case as if the charges against both of them were indisputable and obvious. He managed to get a great deal of exposure for the Gilliver name and Sylvia Gilliver Boggs' interests. For her part, Sylvia showed little expression but secretly harbored a growing sympathy for Charlie, mostly. *What if he hadn't rescued Grace?*

Brian Boggs, like Evans, said the case was black and white. After the second day of trial, Sylvia confessed her sympathies to him over dinner.

Brian was speechless, momentarily. He cleared his throat. "Sylvia," he said, "these are the people who've been taking care of your niece for seven years. Those are years that you, or we, didn't have her in our family."

"That's what bothers me, what you said. Taking care. Grace was in good hands, whether we knew it or not. Now, this precious little girl has been in a foster home for nearly a year. She must be suffering!"

"Oh, for crying out loud, Sylvia. This is what you wanted, isn't it? Remember, you're the one who started this whole thing."

"And, even if they didn't harm her, you know and they know, they should've reported finding her from the beginning. So, you need to swallow your emotions. It's too late now."

Brian stood, pushing his chair back roughly and throwing his napkin down. "I'm going to the office," he said. "I still have work to do. This little legal exercise has taken so much of my time, and now you're having second thoughts. I'm sorry, darling; I need to get away for a while."

Sylvia stared at him. As he walked away, she hungered for someone to share her feelings.

The final witness on the final day was Grace Gilliver Richards, aka Amy Jericho. The Court had deliberated long about the propriety of bringing in an eight-year-old to testify. In the end, after the judge met with her privately, he decided to allow it. He decided the jury needed to hear what she had to say.

Jonathan Lee, Amy's *guardian ad litem*, insisted she be allowed to see Mae and Charlie before her testimony, thinking the shock of seeing each other for the first time in nearly a year would be too emotional for all parties involved. Evans objected because of the possibility of undue influence on the witness. Hamilton and Noonis went along with Lee's reasoning. At last they were granted a ten-minute meeting in a brief court recess before Amy's scheduled appearance with all parties present.

Amy bounded immediately into Charlie's arms as he knelt to embrace her. "Daddy, Daddy," Amy cried. "I thought those bad people hurt you. I'm so glad you're not dead!"

"Me too, honey," Charlie said.

Amy turned to Mae and covered her wet face with kisses. "Mommy! I missed you! Why did they take me away? I don't understand." Amy cried.

"I don't—" Mae started. All four attorneys in the room signaled for her to stop. She hugged Amy, tenderly drying her tears with her finger. "Look how much you've grown, honey. We missed you too. Tell us how you've been—how are you doing in school?"

Charlie stroked Amy's hair but she became suddenly, uncharacteristically shy. "Okay," she said. She turned and buried her face in Charlie's shirt.

"That's enough," Evans said, looking at his watch. "Time's up."

"So soon?" A flash of panic crossed Mae's face. She composed herself with difficulty. "Amy, remember we love you and we always will. Nothing can change that."

Amy moved woodenly as her *guardian ad litem* took her away, but at the door she looked back and smiled. Charlie and Mae were watching her with affection in their eyes, holding hands.

Amy's testimony was very brief. She whispered at first, but soon showed the spark of her natural pluckiness to the delight of everyone in the courtroom. Except Evans.

Sylvia sat transfixed and memorized every detail of the little girl's features and movements. *There is no doubt this is Lisa's child. My God, she could be Lisa, thirty years ago.* Sylvia shivered.

Evans insisted on addressing the young witness as Grace, but every time the child said, "My name is Amy." Evans indulged this with one of his patronizing gestures and condescending smiles, but if he was trying to show how brain-washed she'd been, he failed in the attempt. Amy was articulate and charming. *The little lawyer–like her mother,* Sylvia became ruefully aware.

"Now Grace," Evans said.

"Amy."

"Okay. I'll go along with it for purposes of these proceedings only. Can you point, young lady, to your father, if he's in the courtroom?"

"No," Amy said.

"No?"

"Mommy told me it's not polite to point."

The spectators tittered.

"Oh, she did, did she?"

"Yes sir."

"Well, in that case, can you point to your Mommy, if she's in this room if I give you permission to point?"

"She's right there." Amy jumped up and waved at Mae who fluttered her fingers in acknowledgment.

Sylvia observed the unspoken affection between Grace and Charlie and Mae as Grace answered the few questions from the defense counsel. When the bailiff led the child out, she broke away and ran to hug Charlie. The judge struck his gavel and announced a fifteen-minute recess.

Sylvia turned toward her husband, Brian, sitting beside her, startled at the sight of his face. Deathly pale, covered with perspiration and tear-stained.

Deliberations took longer than anyone expected. Charlie and Mae huddled in a corner booth in the coffee shop across the street from the courthouse.

"She looked good, didn't she?" Charlie asked. "Our Amy."

Mae had a wistful expression. "A bit taller and much thinner, I'd say, but, yes, she still is our beautiful girl."

Their attorneys sat at an adjacent table, gulping sandwiches as they thumbed through papers and made the occasional note, saying little. A few of the courtroom spectators stared at Mae and Charlie. Some smiled and nodded in their direction.

"I guess it's up to the jury now," Charlie said.

"Nate said the judge is the one who decides the sentences."

Charlie's heart wavered, looking at his wife's guileless blue eyes, but he said nothing.

"Oh, Charlie, how I wish this wasn't happening to us." Mae clutched his hand. Her hand in his felt very warm, feverish.

"It's too late now," Charlie said.

When the Court reconvened, Sylvia could hardly breathe. Beyond a doubt, Grace, her sister Lisa's daughter, was alive and had been before her in the witness stand. She also had a rueful knowledge perhaps Grace did belong with the family who had raised her thus far. *But, the child is a Gilliver. Can't I offer her so much more? And what does Brian really feel? Want?*

The jury foreman answered in a clear voice when called upon to read their verdict. Both Charlie and Mae were found guilty of a class two felony, non-aggravated kidnapping. No mandatory sentence because the child had not been confined against her will. Mae was also found guilty of creating false documents, a class three forgery felony. They both were pasty-faced and confused as they conferred with their respective lawyers. The judge set the sentencing hearing for the following week and released the defendants on their personal recognizance.

Sylvia felt flush with victory, then cold with realization. Regardless of their sentencing, Charlie and Mae were now convicted felons. This could only add to their troubles. Plus the custody case loomed after the resolution of this case. As felons, Charlie and Mae could hardly prove fitness, even though they were *de facto* foster parents. *Could they?*

As they were herded out of Court by their attorneys, she began to formulate a plan.

14

Provenance

"Money is NOT the object," Leland said with a sly glance at Brian and a nod toward Brian's desk. The hidden tape recorder was engaged and both men knew it. "Or, maybe it is, considering how much the developer of that land stands to make."

Brian sat at his desk fingering the envelope inside his jacket. *Is now the time?* He cleared his throat. "Well, perhaps it will take a little more than money to convince Marsh to sell the property." He took the envelope out and laid it on the table but rested his hand on top of it.

Leland winked and leaned back in his chair, crossing his arms over his chest. "What the hell does that mean?"

Brain sat a bit straighter. "Now that you mention it, this is worth more than money, at least to Marsh Dalton."

Leland's eyebrows shot up.

"Not that we would do anything with this information other than report it, I mean. Only Marsh knows the full truth."

"You son-of-a-bitch, quit playing games with me."

Leland scooped up the envelope and pulled out the two folded pages of legal-sized paper it contained. His eyes swept the first page but slowed and stopped as he stared at the second one. Leland's eyes grew wide and his complexion chalky.

"That bastard," Leland said. "The implications are–if you can prove any of this…"

"Exactly," Brian said. "The implications are…"

Leland was grim as he finished Brian's sentence.

"Murder."

Sergeant Andrews frowned at his reflection in the slate-shadowed glass of evening in his office window. For a long moment, he rubbed his temples with his fingertips. Sighing, he turned back to the single sheet of paper on his desk. The clipped words were pasted upon the page. He reread them a dozen times.

BANKER DOESN'T WANT TO SHOW

SECRET THINGS THAT YOU SHOULD KNOW

THERE MIGHT BE ANOTHER CRIME

HIDDEN IN HIS DOWNWARD LINE

Andrews scratched his chin and rubbed his temples again. It was late. He shoved the note into his top desk drawer and locked it. Grabbing his jacket with one hand, he reached for the cord to his window blinds with the other. *Enough is enough. I can't think about this anymore tonight.*

He opened the door as he flipped off the light switch. He started at the sight of the figure standing before him in the gloomy hallway. He had never seen this person look as disheveled and sloppy as he did now.

"Sergeant, I must speak with you," Marsh Dalton said. "Someone is blackmailing me."

Andrews filled the crusty, overworked Mr. Coffee in his office for a fresh pot. He concealed his surprise at seeing Marsh Dalton in a state of disarray.

Marsh sat in the chair in front of Andrews' desk and did not appear to be looking at anything in particular. Andrews poured two cups of coffee and sat down, pushing one cup across his desktop toward the older man.

"Thanks," Marsh said. Andrews noticed Marsh's hand was trembling.

"Sergeant, I've always been a contributing member of this community, haven't I?"

"Yes sir."

"Well, in so far as you know, anyway. You're too young to remember me in my early days, thank God."

Andrews lifted an eyebrow but said nothing.

"Somebody does remember though. Somebody's blackmailing me about something that should remain dead and buried." Marsh stared vacantly into space for a moment, then repeated, "Dead and buried."

Andrews pressed his lips together. "Mr. Dalton," he said. "Obviously there must be an element of truth involved or else there wouldn't be blackmail. If you've come to file a complaint, it may require revealing that truth."

"You ever make a mistake, Sergeant?" Marsh asked.

"Let's stick to the point."

"Well, that is the point, as I see it. I made a mistake when I was young and foolish. But I've been paying for it all my life. You have to admit I've done very well, financially speaking."

Andrews felt a tug of impatience. "I wouldn't know," he said.

"Of course you would! I'm one of Tillman's leading citizens. My name is always in the news for this or that contribution."

"Your point?"

Marsh's voice was tinged with condescension. "My point, sir, is now I expect some service, some consideration for all I've done for this community. I want you to find this rotten SOB and make him stop before…"

"Before what?"

"Oh!" Marsh seemed momentarily confused. "Oh, nothing. What I mean is I'll file charges. I'll get the best lawyer money can buy." He got his second wind. "I want this stopped and now or I'll take some other kind of action." He slammed his fist on the desktop causing his coffee to splash over the side of his Styrofoam cup.

Andrews regarded Marsh. In spite of his uncharacteristic rumpled appearance, he had regained his usual bullying forcefulness. Andrews leaned forward, pointing a finger directly at Marsh.

"Is that some kind of threat, Mr. Dalton? Because I don't take kindly to it. This is the first I've heard of what you're calling blackmail. What exactly do you want me to do?"

"Why stop it, of course. Catch the creep."

"Then start at the beginning and tell me everything. That's the only way we can help you." As Andrews unlocked his top desk drawer and pulled out a blank pad of paper, he caught a glimpse of the note he had placed there earlier. *At least I know who that's about now. What's the crime he's trying to hide?*

Andrews sat tapping his pencil.

"When you get old enough to pay for everything you want," Marsh said, "you find you don't want as much." He snickered. "Or, it can't be bought. You know what I mean?"

"Not exactly." Andrews' response was cool.

"Well, I'd like to tell you a story but there are parts of it I don't know how to explain. Especially to you. To the law, I mean."

Andrews sat straighter. "Try me."

"Years ago, when I was very young, I was in love." Marsh coughed.

Andrews nodded.

"We were foolish and made some mistakes, but we were so much in love. She got pregnant and I panicked. I turned my back on her and left her to fend for herself. It's the greatest, well almost the greatest, regret of my life."

"Mr. Dalton, I'm not sure where you're going with this."

Marsh held his hand up. "Here's the point, Sergeant. She had a baby. A boy, my son. I wanted so much to hold him and to take care of them both. But, well these days it doesn't matter as much—the color of her skin. She could pass. That one. Rachel. God she was beautiful." Marsh became dreamy-eyed for a moment.

Andrews waited.

"I couldn't marry a negress, Sergeant. Certainly you can understand."

"Surely you're not the only one to find himself in that situation." Andrews was repulsed but tried to sound kind.

"Surely. But here's the thing. The child needed care. He was defective and had some kind of disability. Can you imagine? My son, defective? Anyway, I refused to claim him and turned my back on her. I managed to go away to school and put them both out of my thoughts, for years."

"Now, someone has apparently found out and I'm being black-mailed. I can't even begin to understand how it happened. After all these years." Marsh shook his head.

"Mr. Dalton," Andrews said. "This is a serious charge, if it can be proved. Please give me the details, and I'll file a report and begin the investigation."

Marsh told him about the phone calls and the threats.

"Get Greene on the line," Leland barked into the speaker phone.

"He's in committee now," the secretary said. "His staff won't interrupt him."

"You can tell them a thing or two from me," Leland bel-lowed. "Any contributions he thought he was getting from GillRich Construction he can kiss goodbye. And he might have to answer to me anyway." Leland stabbed the button on the phone to turn it off.

Brian sat fidgeting in front of Leland's huge desk. "It might be best not to say anything possibly construed as a threat."

"Threat my ass." Leland paced now. "He's double-crossed us, that's what. Why, he told me the earmark money was as good as in the bank." Leland stopped after he'd said the word bank. "Wonder how our banker friend is taking this?" he asked. "It's his secret."

"And he's kept it for over forty years," Brian said.

"Well, damn it." Leland fumed. "We might as well close shop on the new project." He squinted at Brian. "How is it you didn't see this coming?"

Brian squirmed in his chair, rose and walked to the liquor cabinet in Leland's office. "May I?" he asked, picking up a decanter.

"Hell, why not?" Leland flopped back into his desk chair. "All you're good for is drinking my best whiskey and draining me dry with your legal fees."

Brian's hand shook as he poured. "Now, Leland, who could've foreseen this turn of events from the State Legislature?"

"Isn't that what we pay lobbyists for?"

"Sure, but that do-gooder on the appropriations committee insisted on a new survey, and that could've been fixed if the Shawnee hadn't picked this very inopportune time to flood."

Leland smashed his fist down on the desktop. "Damn it, damn it, damn it. All these months of work for nothing. At least I have satisfaction knowing Marsh is getting screwed too. Hah! He won't be able to keep his little secret much longer."

"True, it's practically ready to rip now, but here's the thing. He's a nervous wreck. I wouldn't be surprised if he has a stroke."

"Well, whatever," Leland said. He strode to the liquor cabinet for his bourbon, neat. "You'd better make damn sure this company disappears now. With no trails to me."

"Or me," Brian said. He didn't say he was already thinking how well this whole setback was turning to his advantage.

Andrews began to think of his retirement, though he was too young. The unraveling of Marsh Dalton had shocked him and made him question the truth of everything else he knew. He recalled the banker's words verbatim, going over them again and again in his mind, grasping for trust in his own senses.

He didn't have to search long for clues to the blackmail. As soon as Marsh left his office, the editor of the *Tillman Tattler* had called. "I think you should see this."

Anonymous delivery to the newspaper of copies of forty-year-old hospital records, including a birth certificate, had indeed revealed Marsh's dark secret. But it was not his darkest.Marsh did not show up at the bank the following morning. Most unusual. Andrews had called there and also called Marsh's house with no luck. As he was leaving his office for lunch, he nearly tripped over a straggly man sitting on the hallway floor. *How did he get here?*

Andrews then took a step back when the man looked up and he recognized Marsh Dalton.

"Mr. Dalton," Andrews said, extending his hand to help the man stand, noting how old he unexpectedly seemed.

"Sergeant," Marsh said. "You have to talk to me."

"Well, yes, there is something new regarding the matter we talked about last night. Please come into my office."

Marsh tottered to his feet and shuffled into Andrews' office, then slouched immediately into the nearest chair. His perfect silver hair stuck out in back and the hollows under his eyes were purple. He smelled unwashed.

"Forget that blackmail stuff, Sergeant," Marsh said, gesturing six feet back toward the hallway. "You might want to shut the door."

Andrews tapped it shut with one finger, stepped behind his desk and composed his surprise.

"It's all true," Marsh said. "So I don't care anymore if they print it or not. I'll never sleep again, either way."

Andrews took the printed note from his top drawer along with a blank pad of paper. "Seems the culprit wanted us to suspect you of something else too." He shoved the paper across his desk toward Marsh. "But now you say—"

"That's right." Marsh swept the note away and it floated to the floor. "It's all true."

"Mr. Dalton, last night I received a call from the editor of the *Tillman Tattler*. They received an anonymous tip, a copy of an old birth certificate naming you as the father of one Charlie D. Jericho. You told me about your son but is he the Charlie Jericho who's been on trial for kidnapping? Are you telling me that's true?"

"Yes, yes, Sergeant, that's what I'm saying. It doesn't matter who knows now. My life is gone. At least I changed my will to give it all to the boy."

"Mr. Dalton, I think you might be overreacting. Fathering a child out of wedlock is not, in itself, a crime."

"No." Marsh hung his head between drooping shoulders. "But killing his mother is."

Andrews felt his stomach drop. Could he possibly have heard right? Marsh's bloodshot eyes swiveled around the room, unfocused, when he'd raised his head. Andrews regarded him with a new perspective.

Is this man drugged? Or insane? He pushed a button on his phone and called for a back-up police officer.

"What's that?" Marsh asked.

"I have to advise you," he said, "Mr. Dalton, you have certain rights and before we say anything else, I'd like to have a witness present."

"Whatever. It doesn't make any difference."

The two men sat in silence for a few moments, and a dreamy look came into Marsh's eyes. The officer came in and stood against the wall. Marsh didn't seem to notice.

"See, I was in love. I told you yesterday, remember?"

Andrews nodded. "Go on."

"But it wasn't going to work out. Rachel wanted to get married and have me support the baby, the defective little boy who was, is, my son. We quarreled, and I hit her—" Marsh broke down in tears.

"Mr. Dalton, I must advise you."

Marsh jumped to his feet. "She didn't get up! Don't you understand? I killed her. And I hid her body and got as far away from Tillman as I could."

Andrews nodded at the officer who read Miranda rights to Marsh.

"Now that boy has all kinds of problems, and it's all my fault. I've tried to watch him, from a distance, of course, all these years, but I can never make up for killing his mother. I know that." He flopped down on the chair again. "Strange. It feels almost good to say it, after all these years." Marsh began to hum.

"Mr. Dalton, before we go any further, call your attorney. This officer will take you to a conference room and stay with you until your attorney comes. We can talk again then."

Marsh stood and shuffled toward the door without a word. The officer grabbed his elbow and led him out.

Andrews rubbed his temples. *Marsh could just be crazy and babbling, but if what he said is true, where did he hide the body?*

15

Confrontation

Jimmy Noble charged through the kitchen and back door of the café into the alley. For days he'd had the creepy feeling someone was following him. He arranged a couple of empty packing crates on top of each other and an inch or two from the outer brick wall of the building so he could stand next to them, unseen in the shadows. The space between the crates and the wall gave him a perfect view of the sidewalk in front of the café as it adjoined the alleyway. He knew he had only moments before his stalker would realize Jimmy wasn't inside and would likely come back to the sidewalk to look for him.

Sure enough, at the edge of the building's shade, Jimmy saw black crepe-soled shoes near the corner. Then he saw Mike Sanders' face clearly illuminated in the flash of his lighter as he paused to light a cigarette and look around. *Come on, you jerk. Step into the alley. A little bit closer now.*

As if summoned, Mike turned to walk through the alley, passing in front of the crates. Jimmy held his breath, waiting for the perfect position, then pushed the top crate over onto Mike, crashing it into his head.

"What the—" Mike shouted, stumbling to his knees. Jimmy jumped onto his back shoving Mike's face into the cinders and stepping onto one of his hands. Jimmy picked up Mike's still lit cigarette and held the burning end only inches from Mike's stunned eyes.

"Listen asshole and listen well. You make one sound and I'm shoving this into your eye. You tell me, right here and right now, who hired you to follow me?"

The answer came in a mumble. "I don't know what..."

Jimmy thrust the burning cigarette close enough to Mike's eye to singe his eyelashes. Mike tried to jerk his head back as he blinked, his eye gushing tears down his cheek.

"I mean it, scumbag," Jimmy said, pulling Mike's head back by his hair.

Mike sputtered and coughed. "Old man," he said.

"Who?" Jimmy ground Mike's hand further into the cinders under his heel.

"Richards."

"Leland Richards? I don't believe you. Why?"

"He still thinks you killed his son." Mike picked the wrong time to smirk.

Jimmy jumped up and kicked Mike in the ribs as hard as he could. "You lying SOB. You're the one who killed him. I know it!"

Mike grabbed his side and vomited.

Behind him, Jimmy had attracted some attention from passersby.

He turned on his heel, sprinted in the opposite direction and left Mike Sanders lying in his own vomit, swirling through the alley cinders.

"I didn't expect to see you again," Brian said, swallowing hard.

Mike Sanders had stepped from the lengthening purple shadows of evening directly into Brian's path as he left his office building. The side of Mike's face was scratched and blackened and his clothing smelled putrid, disgusting.

Brian checked around. The dusky sidewalk was empty.

"Surprise, lawyer man," Mike said, moving closer as Brian recoiled from the smell.

"What do you want?"

"I just lost one of my sources of income, if you know what I mean."

"I can't help you." Brian stepped aside to walk around him and hurried away, but within a few paces he felt his left arm being grabbed and twisted behind his back. Mike shoved him into a dark vestibule.

"I think you can," he said.

Brian struggled to fight off nausea he felt from the smell. *So this is his MO. Well, I'm not some helpless old man.* Brian dropped his suitcase, thrust his right elbow backwards into Sanders' side, but the man was too fast. He swerved and grabbed Brian's right arm too.

"Forget it man." Mike's laugh was cynical. "We need to talk."

"Look, there's nothing to talk…" The grip on Brian's arm tightened sharply. "Okay. Okay. Not here though. Not now. Let me go and I promise we'll go somewhere to talk."

Mike loosened his hold. "Where?"

"Somewhere–close."

Mike released Brian's arms. Relief flooded his body as Brian shook out his arms and thought frantically of a place where he wouldn't be seen talking to Mike. "I'm headed toward the parking garage. Meet me in there in five minutes, but don't walk with me." *It should be deserted now.*

Mike stood back as Brian bent to retrieve his briefcase and hurried onto the sidewalk. "Remember I know where you live, lawyer man."

Brian flinched but kept moving. As he rushed into the parking garage, his thoughts tumbled furiously. *Maybe I can get rid of two problems at once.* He quickened his pace. With a monogrammed handkerchief he wiped away the perspiration on his brow and struggled to swallow rising bile.

Full shadows cast from cylindrical support columns were diminished by sallow rays of yellow light from the row of tiny light fixtures set into the ceiling. He craned his neck to look in every direction as he slowed his pace toward his car.

When he turned and leaned against his classic Jaguar XKE, he was immediately assaulted by the stench announcing the presence of Mike Sanders. Brian jumped, and looking down at Mike's dirty black shoes, he realized Mike hadn't waited, as instructed, but had been only a few silent steps behind him.

Now he used the handkerchief to cover his nose and mouth as he prepared his practiced, impassive lawyer face. He scanned the area again before he spoke, his voice low, measured and slow.

"Listen well. There is a job you can do for me, but I'm only going to say this once and then I'm leaving. Understand?"

Mike grinned and winked.

Looking at him, Brian fought a wave of nausea but continued in the same measured voice. "There are some houses, down by the railroad tracks on Sparrow Street. Know the place?"

Mike narrowed his eyes but nodded.

"Well, they're mostly old and some are unoccupied. It wouldn't surprise anyone if one started on fire, and maybe spread to the others. Do you get my meaning?"

"Piece of cake," Mike said. "But it sounds kind of expensive, if you get my meaning."

Brian's anger surged as he looked at the filthy, grinning man. *How dare he threaten me?*

"Look," he said. "$5,000 when the job's done. Take it or leave it."

"No way. That's chicken feed."

Brian dodged sideways to get to his car door but Sanders stepped closer, pinning Brian against his car. Sanders slurred his speech.

"I need cash now so open your pockets, lawyer man."

"Certainly not," Brian said. He gagged and struggled to keep panic from overcoming him. *This creep might kill me! Got to think!*

"Hey, you there!" The shout came from across the parking garage. Jimmy Noble could clearly see Mike Sanders pressing himself against Brian and ran toward them.

"Shit," Mike said. In one quick motion, he reached inside his jacket, pulled out a knife and drove it upwards into Brian's chest. "I've always hated you. I'm through with you, man."

He dropped his grasp on Brian and sprinted away.

Brian looked down at the blood gushing from his ribcage. *Oh God. Fuck.*

He fumbled open his briefcase, thrashing his hand around inside for the pistol. *Yes!* Steadying his arm across the roof of his car, he pulled the trigger as many times as he could before black spots filled his vision, and he fell backward.

Brian didn't hear or see Mike stumble and skid across the cement floor on his face.

Jimmy arrived in time to hear his last words before giving him CPR.

"Mike Sanders."

At Mercy Hospital's intensive care unit, a specialized nurse sponged perspiration from Mike Sanders' forehead with tentative touches as he thrashed from side to side. Within moments, she pulled the thick blankets up to his neck, careful to circumvent the multiple tubes attached to his arms as he shivered. His teeth rattled and chattered. She resumed her seat, close to his side, waiting for the chill to pass.

In spite of the tube inserted down his throat, Mike began to smack his lips together and wag his thick, coated tongue. She slipped a tiny ice chip into his mouth.

Soon he stopped but began tensing his throat in a contorted effort to speak. The nurse leaned closer as he whispered, "His fault." He stopped and looked at the nurse.

"Whose fault?" she asked.

"Boggs," Mike said, suddenly lucid. "He wanted me to burn."

"Burn?"

"Houses. With people in them." Mike's confession was interrupted by a coughing fit in which his sputum was punctuated with tiny droplets of blood. After several painstaking minutes of sipping more water, he spoke again. "Wanted them gone. Double-crossed me." More coughing. More blood.

"Perhaps you shouldn't talk now, Mr. Sanders," the nurse said. She motioned to the deputy on the other side of the bullet-proof glass that separated the patients from the observation area for Donna Sanders to come in. Even a criminal under arrest got to see family when he was critically injured. It was time for her five minutes per hour.

"No," Mike said with some force as Donna took her seat opposite the nurse. The women responded with wide eyes and raised eyebrows.

"Your wife is here now, Mr. Sanders."

His eyes flickered in Donna's direction, and then returned to the nurse's face. "Ask her. She knows about the river cabin–how to get in." He coughed again, but grasped the nurse's hand. With effort he resumed his thick-tongued talk. "I wasn't gonna do it. But he owed me money."

The nurse gave Donna a nervous glance. "Do you want to tell this to the police?"

"Yeah," Mike said. "He shouldn't get away..." He began to thrash back and forth, perspiring again and whispering "Lillian," the name of his deceased baby daughter.

The nurse tried to still him and began sponging again. "You'd better go now," she said gesturing sideways across the bed, but Donna Sanders was already gone.

The iron anvil of despair settled upon Sylvia's chest. She alternated between sucking in great gulps of air and being unable to breathe.

Sitting on her living room sofa, she gave up all pretense of poise and hung her head between her knees to combat dizziness. *Brian's dead!*

"Take your time, ma'am," Sergeant Andrews said. His voice sounded garbled to her, as if under water. "We only have a few questions at this time."

Straightening, she accepted a glass of cold water from Marianna whose red-eyed, tear-streaked face hovered in and out of focus before her. A wave of numbness flooded over her, and she was conscious of her extremities feeling very cold. After several minutes, she nodded at the officers.

Andrews began, in a gentle voice. "I have to ask you, Mrs. Boggs, do you know a man by the name of Mike Sanders?"

Sylvia's head hurt like her brain had been sand-blasted. She hesitated. "No. No, I don't ... wait a minute. That name does sound familiar. Wasn't he one of the firemen injured in the train crash that killed my sister?"

"I believe so, yes."

"He might have had some dealings with my husband–something about a lawsuit. I think I heard Brian mention his name once or twice, but I don't know the man." At the sound of her own voice speaking her husband's name, Sylvia erupted with tears and soon, uncontrollably hiccupped with sobs.

Andrews spoke softly. "That's all, ma'am. We'll be back in touch tomorrow and leave you alone for now."

Sylvia's vision blurred. Her shoulders shook. *Alone. Yes, there's no one I can call. I am utterly and completely alone.*

Shock waves reverberated through the courtroom when news spread of the murder of Brian Boggs. Sylvia's absence was like a gaping open wound, an invisible presence adding pain to already painful proceedings.

Hollow-eyed state's attorney Evans pawed through papers seemingly searching for something again and again.

The judge entered and Mae stood on shaky knees. Charlie was wound like a coil ready to spring. He simply couldn't imagine what would happen if they both went to jail, or even if only one of them did. He'd been thinking of his grandmother, Lorraine, so often lately. She would have told him not to be afraid, to do what is right–whatever that was. She also would have told him to pray. And pray he did.

When the judge called his name, he stepped forward with his head held high. The Court bailiff restated the charges against him and the decision of the jury for each one.

The judge said, "Now, Mr. Jericho, once again these are the charges against you and the findings of a jury of your peers. I have discretion to set the degree of your punishment based on these findings. The Class II felony legal statute does not carry a mandatory sentence, so after much deliberation, I hereby sentence you to seven years' probation."

Charlie twisted his head around toward Mae who was staring straight ahead like a lost child. Charlie then turned toward Jed Hamilton, standing next to him, who was smiling broadly but then dropped his head as the judge continued.

"This means you will not be incarcerated but will be under the auspices of the Court. Should you be involved in any criminal activity or any trouble of any kind, the terms of your probation will be considered violated, and you will be remanded to the Court, which may decide that your sentence, or any portion thereof remaining, would be best served out in confinement. Do you understand?"

Charlie nodded. "Yes, your Honor. Thank you. I won't get in any more trouble."

Hamilton touched Charlie's arm, and he stepped back.

Mae trembled when her name was called, and Nate Noonis held her elbow as he stepped forward with her. "Mrs. Jericho," the judge said. "You also have heard the charges against you and the jury's decision. Your actions, the Court feels, are more egregious than those of your husband's because you knowingly falsified records in order to keep up the pretense of legitimately having a child. Because of this and your added responsibilities as a mandated reporter, which you breached, it is the considered opinion of this Court that you should be sentenced to sixty days at county and ten years' probation."

Mae gasped and wobbled, pressing her palm onto the small of her back. Noonis supported her. Charlie felt hot tears spring up and he blinked furiously to contain them.

"This means," the judge said, "after your period of incarceration, you will remain under the Court's supervision for the remainder of your sentence, and any legal infraction on your part shall result in the appropriate punishment. Do you understand?"

Mae squeaked a polite affirmation. As her blue eyes sought Charlie's face, her attorney whispered to her and the bailiff led her away.

The industrial grey inside the county jail seemed to seep into Mae's very bones. Clutching the thin blanket in her fists at night, she closed her eyes and tried to pray. But she truly didn't remember how. *Charlie is praying for me though, I know.*

Her warm home, the simple home-cooked meals Charlie made and the whole idea of a family haunted her days. She ate little, fought nausea and told no one of her stomach and back pains, thinking them the result of sorrow and bad food. No one made eye contact with her after glimpsing the dark circles in her thinning face. Only the matron took notice when Mae awoke fitful and moaning in a pool of her own blood.

Life Wish

Charlie visited Mae every day for as long as he was allowed. Together they faced the ordeal of testing and treatment, during which Mae was transported to Mercy Hospital, where she had worked for so many years. Crystal managed to finagle her way to see Mae, and the two women hugged each other and cried together.

"Mae," Crystal said.

"No. There's no need now."

"But I have to say how sorry I am. About the way things turned out with Amy. If I had known…"

Mae shushed her with a wave of her hand. "I've had plenty of time to think, and now I know, or at least I think I know, what forgiveness means. I've had to forgive everyone, Crystal, but no one more than myself."

"You were always so good to that child. And to Charlie. And the patients all loved you. It doesn't seem right that you are suffering so much now."

Mae sighed. "It isn't easy to go through all this but like I said, I've had time to think. And to pray. Crystal, I do pray now. Every day. It's too late, the doctors tell me—"

"Oh I don't believe that. Surely there's something—"

"No, no. If they find some treatment or a miracle cure, I'll be grateful, but I was wrong, Crystal. From the beginning. I wanted a child so much I turned a blind eye to the truth. I thought, together with Charlie, we could keep Amy and no one would ever find out. I was selfish and foolish and cruel." Mae started to cry.

Crystal put her arms around her. "Amy was your greatest blessing, honey, and also your greatest test, I guess. But she was lucky to have a happy family and to have your love for however long it was."

Mae smiled and kissed Crystal on the cheek before being wheeled away for therapy.

16

Reckoning

Brian's funeral was politely attended by the more prominent citizens of Tillman. Most stayed only long enough to sign the register and say a few words to Sylvia, but some lingered to listen or to gossip in whispers.

Leland Richards felt no compunction to socialize. He sat alone, head down, eyes closed. Others may have thought he appeared to be praying, but he was going over in his mind the mistakes he'd made with Brian. He couldn't decide whether Brian had been so monumentally stupid or if he, himself, was even more stupid for having trusted him.

Their wild speculator's scheme had collapsed. It may not have succeeded even if Brian had lived since Senator Greene had not been able to deliver on his legislative promises for the windfall funding. Come to think of it, he'd heard the Senator's voice a moment ago. Leland opened one eye and turned his head slightly. Greene's back was to him as the Senator shook hands with Sylvia standing beside the closed casket.

"Humph." Leland murmured, turning back to his thoughts. *How could Brian have double-crossed him? Greedy bastard. Wonder how much more he got out of Marsh? Poor devil.*

His heart ached for Sylvia, and he suppressed his own dismay at learning that Grace was not his biological granddaughter. *In my lifetime, this is the saddest tangle of events I've ever seen.* Lifting one eye open again, he saw Sylvia still standing at the front of the room, a vision of dignity and poise.

Jimmy and Nora Noble approached her, shook hands and offered their condolences. He was pretty sure Sylvia didn't know them personally, but she was gracious and warm. Jimmy had tried to save Brian, after all, and had identified his murderer. Leland mused; to think all these years he'd blamed Jimmy for Ben's death. Again, he closed his eyes and shook his head. *So wrong.*

Sighing deeply, Leland had sudden clarity. He'd step down from the chairmanship of the GillRich Board. Having made that decision, he felt lighter, freer.

Straightening and looking forward, he suppressed a smile. With Brian gone, he'd extricate himself, quietly, from every contract and business deal that involved him or his paper company. Sure, he'd take a loss, but he'd still have more than enough money. Then when he abandoned the leadership at GillRich, he'd be free to spend more time with Grace, if possible. Perhaps he could turn his life around. In silence, he rose from the pew and went to stand by Sylvia.

Thomas Eikens shuffled through the foyer extending greetings to several people he knew. The atmosphere had a surreal quality, and he felt like he was dreaming.

"Yes," he said, shaking the hands of two board members. "Brian's death seems impossible, especially under the circumstances."

"Leland is sitting with his head down in one of the front pews," said one of the men. "He may be particularly shattered by this and, between you and me, I wonder at his ability to continue to lead GillRich."

Thomas squinted in Leland's direction, but his eyes glassed over with tears when he saw Sylvia. *How much more could the woman take?* Refocusing on Leland, he shook his head. "That remains to be seen, gentlemen."

"Well," the other man whispered. "We don't want you to be surprised when we nominate you to become Chairman of the Board at the meeting next month. Leland has served long and well, but it seems the right time to move on and take a new direction."

They both nodded. "Several others agree with us, Thomas," one said. "You're the most capable, now that Marsh is out of the equation."

"Is he here?" Thomas asked.

"No. As far as we know he's in jail. Even if he was out, I doubt he'd show his face here."

Thomas slouched. "You're probably right. It's still hard to believe what he's done, even if it was so long ago. We were close business colleagues for all these years, and I'd never have guessed his secrets."

Moving on to greet others, Thomas began to feel his courage wane as he got closer to Sylvia. He'd intended to tell her how sorry he was, but it all made sense to him now. All the attacks and vandalism had been the result of Brian's shady associations. That didn't seem appropriate to mention at this venue.

Nearing the place where Sylvia stood, he saw Leland step to her side. *Great. Now I'm forced to speak to him too.* Sylvia's hand flew to her collar in a nervous gesture, and Thomas had to offer her whatever comfort he could.

He came to Leland first but did not extend his hand. "Sad day," he said.

Leland was in a distant place, but seeing Thomas, he reached out to hug him.

Thomas stepped back, startled.

"Thomas, I'm so sorry for all the bad blood that's gone between us," Leland said.

"Bad blood? That's what you call it?"

"Yes. I've been a conniving old fool for so long. This man's death," he gestured toward Brian's coffin, "has shown me how wrong I've been."

"Well, it will take much more to convince me you didn't know what you were doing when you manipulated the board into land speculation, among other things. What you do now will demonstrate how much you've changed, if at all."

Leland swallowed hard. "I know it won't be easy, but I'll prove it to you and to everyone else in this town. In fact, I'm recommending you to take over the chairmanship of GillRich's board, Thomas."

Thomas remained silent, wondering at the coincidence of hearing that suggestion two times in only a few minutes. Then he moved away from Leland to extend his condolences to Sylvia.

Sergeant Andrews sat in a somber corner of a back pew, inconspicuous in his faded brown suit. The citizens of Tillman were used to seeing him in uniform and most would probably not give him a second glance today.

This was good. It afforded him the opportunity to watch while virtually unobserved. He sat with his elbows on his knees, fingertips tented together, wondering what other criminal activities were going on in his town. The past few weeks had been rife with one surprise after another, and Brian's murder was the topper.

Sylvia looked to be holding up well from his vantage point. *Good genes, though her family has been touched by scandal repeatedly.* Thinking of the little girl, Grace or Amy or perhaps he would think of her as Amy-Grace, brought forth a rare smile. His recommendation, strange as it turned out to be, would be for the child to stay with Charlie Jericho and his plucky wife.

Andrews sighed. He sat back, further into the shadows, as Leland Richards slid from his front row pew and approached Sylvia. There were rumors of investment fraud, but he had a feeling Leland would brush off the stain like a wayward crumb. He always did.

Even from the distance, he could see that Leland had a dreamy look about him. *The man must be delusional. Help like his Sylvia doesn't need.* Andrews shook his head to dislodge those thoughts.

Thomas Eikens came into his field of vision. Andrews had always liked him, thought him to be honest and honorable. Too bad he'd suffered so much as the hands of someone like Marsh Dalton.

Dalton had been the biggest surprise to Andrews. Clearly he'd hidden his mental illness for many years, but at this very moment, he sat blubbering in a jail cell, abandoned by his socialite wife and some of these very people who'd been his alleged friends. The search crew for the body Marsh said was buried at the river's overgrown easement, ironically almost directly behind the houses where Charlie Jericho and others had lived, would start tomorrow.

As if summoned, Charlie appeared in the line winding toward Sylvia. *What's he doing here?* Andrews had to admit Charlie looked respectful and subdued. *He must have a very good reason for showing his face here.*

The whispering and furtive glances as well as the open stares Charlie ignored made him sit straighter and feel for the gun inside his suit coat.

Jimmy was still shaken by the demons of his own memory of watching Brian die, but he went to the funeral to attempt some closure. He slumped into such knee-weakening relief that Mike Sanders was in custody he was almost joyful.

At the funeral home, many knew the story and shook his hand or clapped him on the back. Sylvia hugged him, they cried together for a few moments. Her graciousness touched him.

After Nora extended her condolences, she and Jimmy sat at the back of the room.

"It's very odd, Nora," Jimmy said. "This town we live in."

"What do you mean?"

"Less than a week ago, everything was *status quo*. Now Brian's death has blown this town open, and everyone is coming here to seek some kind of an answer. No one wants to miss out on anything."

"That's us too," Nora said.

"Yes, I guess so, but just look at some of these folks. There's Leland Richards up front. He's been acting bereaved, with his head down, but now he's standing next to Sylvia. Wonder if he thinks she'll be his business partner now that Brian's gone?"

"I hope not, for her sake, but I really don't know why. Brian made his business partners look suspicious if only by association."

Jimmy murmured something and jerked his eyes away from Leland and Sylvia. He felt a stab of pride when he saw how humbly Charlie approached the front. Everyone standing near or in the aisle moved back to let him pass.

Charlie put his hand out to Sylvia. There was a collective pause as she hesitated, then an audible exhale as she took it. Despite the silent lull, no one could hear Charlie's low whispers or Sylvia's reply, and even Leland stood aside. Within ninety seconds, Charlie walked out of the room with his head down.

"That looked hopeful," Nora said. "Maybe they will be able to come to an agreement about that lovely child." She turned toward Jimmy. "Amy was the brightest and happiest girl in my class. Anyone could see that she was loved."

"Yeah, well, it still doesn't change what he did, Nora. I hope no one takes advantage of him because he might inherit some money, so the rumor goes. From Marsh."

"Like I said, she's a wonderfully well-adjusted student. They may have come to raise Amy by questionable means, but they can both be proud of the job they've done. She's delightful. Or, should I say, she was delightful. The whole experience might change her, young as she is. I worry about that, about her. Not about all of the crazy adults involved."

Jimmy touched Nora's hand to get her attention. "Check out Sergeant Andrews."

Andrews was sitting almost directly across the room from them, and his eyes were fastened on Sylvia and Leland, who were in a serious conversation. Jimmy had noticed the officer clutch his side when Charlie came into the room. Jimmy made an impulsive decision.

"Stay here a minute," he told Nora. "I'm going to catch Charlie."

Charlie concentrated on his verse as he threaded his way through the visitors gathered in the lobby. *Suffering produces perseverance; perseverance, character, and character, hope.* His nose was cold and his cheeks were hot. He believed his face was red, but he pushed on. The verse was no comfort. *There are times, Lord, when all these old scriptures fill my head and I suppose it's good. But can't there be some times I think only of you? So I don't have to think about where I am or what's happened?*

Pushing open the heavy glass door, Charlie sniffed back tears. Sylvia had actually thanked him! For coming. And for taking such good care of Grace all these years. He shook off his thoughts, but some of them were resting on his shoulder. Looking back, he started. Jimmy Noble stood behind him, touching Charlie's shoulder.

"It's been a long time, Charlie," he said.

Charlie blinked and forced himself to stand a bit taller. "Yes, Jimmy, it has. I don't know what to say to you."

"Well, I know what to say to you. I'm sorry. After the accident at the woodshop I was angry for the longest time. I couldn't forgive you then, but now…" Jimmy's voice lowered as he stepped aside to let a couple pass them on the sidewalk outside the funeral home. "Now, I am proud to have known you and to have been your friend at one time. I'm even thinking maybe we can be friends again."

Charlie stared at Jimmy, open-mouthed. "Did your Dad tell you I came to see you? At the hospital and at home? You never wanted to let me apologize or explain. I never wanted to hurt you, Jimmy."

"It's taken a long time to heal, but I guess I know that now."

Charlie nodded.

"Well, I left my wife inside," Jimmy said. "I wish you the best, old friend." With that, he turned to walk back toward the funeral home.

"Jimmy," Charlie called. "Mae's sick. I guess … I thought you might want to know."

"Sick?"

Charlie nodded.

"Bad?"

"I'm so afraid of losing her, Jimmy. I'm losing my whole family."

Jimmy Noble hugged Charlie. "I'm here for you now. Let us help you."

The two men shook hands and shared a long, silent gaze before Jimmy turned away.

Charlie walked to the memorial garden and sat on a bench to calm himself. Soon he noticed the monument for Lisa Gilliver Richards, Amy's biological mother, with two tiny inscriptions near the base, one for Benjamin John Richards, Jr. and one for Grace Gilliver Richards. *Amy!* Charlie bristled with possessiveness for his daughter, yes, his daughter. That other life that would have been hers ended when the van crashed killing her mother and brother.

He jumped to his feet and hurried off. He didn't want to think of losing Amy again, and he wanted to tell Mae what Sylvia had said to him.

Sylvia's lips felt numb. Too much gracious greeting and not enough time to mentally process everything. She would get through the ordeal of Brian's funeral. There was nothing else to do.

Mr. Willingham approached her and whispered, "It's time."

To her surprise, the chapel was full of people, and although she knew most of them, all their faces blurred before her eyes and she stumbled slightly. Mr. Willingham took her elbow and led her to a private seating area with a large one-way glass window. She was grateful for the solitude and slipped off her shoes to absently rub her feet while she surveyed the faces of the citizens of Tillman crowded into the pews.

How many of them knew the secret she'd only learned recently, the results of his DNA sample, from hairs stolen from his brush. Her fears and suspicions had been so strengthened by Brian's strange behavior she'd taken it upon herself to squash them. She'd hoped for peace of mind, but instead they confirmed her mental anguish. Brian was her niece's biological father. That fact made all of Sylvia's submerged memories burst forth: Brian's eyes following Lisa, Lisa's flirty laughter, Brian's reaction when Lisa's baby daughter's body couldn't be found, Brian's discouragement of her own efforts to find her niece.

Then, suddenly flush with tears, Sylvia recalled how Brian had pressured her to add his name to the title for her home as soon as they returned from their honeymoon. *He only wanted me for my money.* She pursed her lips at the bitter thought. Brian had not wanted Grace even though he'd said he had. But why, if in truth she was his own daughter?

The answer came to her as the organ music ended and a hired preacher prepared to say a few words. *Maybe he didn't know.*

Now fresh sobs escaped and guilt filled her. She went through the motions as she let herself be led to the cemetery, scarcely hearing anything but the blood throbbing in her temples.

In the humid days and airless nights following Brian's funeral, Sylvia moved like a robot through her endless tasks. Brian's personal effects were the easiest to handle. The disposition of his law firm revealed a depth of deception she'd not thought possible of her husband.

Every lucrative Tillman deal had his imprint, and his speculative ventures had stretched the firm's assets to a thin veneer that barely covered the illusion of success.

Particularly difficult was the discovery of his hidden tape recorder which spewed forth privileged details embarrassing to many of his clients. Sylvia flinched when she thought of the tape of Brian and Leland discussing Marsh's blackmail. Bold lies in Brian's voice implicated him, but somehow the tapes absolved Leland—at least of the blackmail. The sly old dog had been careful in his speech, but Brian had deceived him too.

Sylvia was sorry for the employees who'd had to be let go, one by one, as the business of the firm found resolution in the transfer of suits or some other manner. She pitied the clients who'd unwisely depended upon him. Most of all, she tormented herself—for the facts she was now learning. A fool took comfort in knowing she wasn't alone in the duplicity while she was only the most invisible victim.

17

Resolution

"I've lost the will to fight for Grace," Sylvia said. "For her custody."

Ryan H.B. Evans fingered the Waterman pen he held over a yellow legal pad. His pensiveness contrasted with his customary crisp and controlling presence. At long last he sighed, and Sylvia caught a faint whiff of coffee on his breath.

"She never was really mine, and Brian died before he knew about her, uh, paternity." Sylvia leaned her cheek upon her closed hand letting her eyes wander to the view outside. Early summer buzzed with throbbing life around her, and she felt as if she'd come full circle from that May eight years ago when she'd buried her sister and nephew and first learned Grace was missing.

"Well, as you know, Charlie Jericho has come forth with a petition for custody, and Leland Richards would like for you to proceed even though he now knows Grace, or Amy, is not his biological granddaughter. He makes a sentimental but half-hearted plea. Truly, I think the will has gone out of him too."

"For years finding evidence of Grace has been my obsession, and now it's led me to nowhere."

"As a curiosity," Evans asked, "why did you have Brian's DNA tested too?"

"It was his reaction to everything to do with Grace or Lisa. I began to wonder, so I collected several strands from his hairbrush without his knowledge. I'd known he and Lisa were close, from law school I'd thought, but that was before he'd shown interest in me; although we didn't get married until after she–was killed."

Sylvia stifled a sob, then straightened and composed herself. "I do want a meeting with him though. Charlie Jericho. Them, I mean."

Evans raised his eyebrows. "That can probably be arranged. They lost their house, I know, in that east side development fiasco…"

"Please." Sylvia held up her hand. "I don't want to hear anything more about Brian's unscrupulous business deals—"

"No. No. I mean they are living in an apartment across town now, and Charlie was hired by a new woodworking shop on the west side. They are certainly no worse off than before, financially, I mean. Why do you want to meet with them?"

"I want to arrange for Grace's education. I'm assuming they'll get custody, and she's such a bright, precocious little girl. It's the least I can do–to provide for an appropriate education. And, someday, when she's old enough, I'd like for her to know who her family is–the story behind her life. In the meantime, I'd like to visit from time to time. As a friend of the family."

"A tall order, but not one that's impossible, I would think," Evans said. "I'll talk to their attorney and if it goes the way we think it will, I'll see to all the legalities after the custody hearing."

Charlie held Mae's elbow as they walked into the courthouse for the dispositional custody hearing. Neither had ever wanted to go there again, both felt something good would happen today. Charlie carried his head high. Mae wore a brave smile. Neither mentioned Mae's increasing weakness.

Eager to make a good appearance, their attorney, Nate Noonis, positioned them near the front of the Court room. Nate had pledged to do a percentage of his work *pro bono* and could think of no other clients worthier of his sympathies.

Sylvia sat alone a bit farther back and on the other side of the room. Her attorney, Evans, was bent in whispers with Jonathan Lee, Grace's guardian and two case workers from the Department of Child and Family Services.

All stood when the judge entered. "We are here to determine the resolutions before the Court of two petitions for custody of the minor, Grace Gilliver Richards aka Amy Jericho."

"Your Honor," Evans said. "May we approach?" All three attorneys huddled in front of the judge. Charlie saw his eyebrows shoot up before he leaned forward to resume their conversation in whispers. Charlie heard the word "Withdraw" but couldn't make out the rest of the words.

Charlie and Mae's attorney, Nate, wouldn't make eye contact when the attorneys walked back to their places. Evans said, "We hereby request withdrawal of the petition for custody filed by Sylvia Gilliver Boggs."

Charlie and Mae gasped and smiled at each other. *Does this mean? Could it mean?*

Sylvia sat motionless, appearing to be lost in her own thoughts.

"The motion to withdraw the petition for custody filed by Sylvia Gilliver Boggs is hereby granted," the judge said. "That leaves one petition before the Court—that filed on behalf of Charlie and Mae Jericho."

"Your Honor," Jonathan Lee said. "It has come to my attention that these petitioners are not recommended custodians according to the DCFS investigation."

"What?" Charlie asked aloud. Nate warned him to be quiet, and the judge gave him the frown of a strong reprimand. Charlie's lips went numb and his hand throbbed where Mae's fingers dug so tightly into the flesh of his palm. Confusion fell like a blanket around him. He saw that Mae's blue eyes were open wide, sparking with fear.

Lee continued. "You have a copy of their report, your Honor, in which both of the petitioners—"

Evans interrupted. "By both you mean Charlie Jericho and Mae Jericho, correct? To clarify, your Honor."

"Correct," Lee said.

The judge nodded. "Go on."

"According to the DCFS investigation, both Charlie and Mae Jericho are convicted felons. In addition, they have inconsistent means of income."

"That's a lie." Mae blurted this time. "About the income. I'm going back to work as a nurse's aide and Charlie—"

"Mr. Noonis," the judge said to Nate, "I must warn you to tell your clients to show the proper respect for the Court or they'll be removed from these proceedings."

197

Nate gave Mae a pitying look, and Charlie put his arm around her. The glassy pools of her eyes focused straight ahead.

Sylvia motioned to Evans, and their low voices were rasping and sharp.

The judge slammed his gavel. "We'll take a ten minute recess. Counselors, I'll see you in chambers." He stood and stomped away.

The DCFS case workers hurried out of the courtroom, leaving Sylvia, Charlie and Mae alone. Together. For the first time.

Charlie's heart was pounding but he decided to take the first step. He made his way slowly over to where Sylvia sat, her arms crossed and an angry expression on her face. He stuck out his hand, but dropped it back to his side after Sylvia made no move to return the gesture. "I want to thank you, Mrs. Boggs, for backing out of your custody try for Amy," Charlie said.

"Grace," Sylvia hissed. "This was not the way it was supposed to happen."

Her stormy gray eyes reminded Charlie so much of Amy. His voice caught in his throat, and his tumbled thoughts couldn't form words he needed to express himself. After a moment, he shrugged and started back toward Mae.

After the recess, Nate walked toward Charlie and Mae shaking his head. Charlie started to quiver and Mae wobbled and fell backward into her seat. Charlie gripped Mae's hand and held it to his side.

"I've reviewed the DCFS report in full and talked to the attorneys for all parties in chambers," the judge said. "It is the opinion of this Court that the interests of the minor in question would best be protected by placement with an appropriate foster home."

"No!" Mae sputtered through a gush of tears. "I've been in foster homes, and I can't stand the thought of her going to one."

"Well, stand it you must, Mrs. Jericho. You can repetition the Court at a later date when perhaps your circumstances may have changed, but I must tell you that history is against you."

Now Charlie spoke out. "Nobody can love her like we do." Mae sobbed openly.

The judge's annoyance showed in his face. "Do you think, Mr. Jericho, that love alone is sufficient to raise a child? Children must be taught to obey the law too, and you and your wife can hardly demonstrate that—"

Attorney Evans interrupted. "Your Honor, my client, Mrs. Boggs, would like to reinstate her petition for custody of Grace."

"Too late Evans. As I told Noonis' clients, she can re-petition at a later date, and I'll be interested in her motives too for this indecision on her part. As for now, this proceeding is ended." He rammed his gavel down. "The minor Grace Gilliver Richards aka Amy Jericho remains under the custody of the DCFS for appropriate placement in foster care at this time."

Mae wailed. Sylvia hung her head. Charlie threw a fist into the nearest target, his attorney's jaw.

In its wisdom, the Department of Child and Family Services had placed Amy with Nora Noble's neighbor, Trish McGillicutty, another teacher's aide, mandatory reporter and a friend of Nora's.

Trish called Nora at 4:40 p.m. with panic in her voice. "Nora, can you come over right away? I can't find Amy." Nora was out the door within seconds.

"Everything was fine when we got home from school," Trish said. "Amy went into her bedroom to play, and I went into mine to change clothes before going to the kitchen to make her afterschool snack. She loves peanut butter on crackers with milk."

"How long before you went to Amy's room?" Nora asked as both women searched every space of the modest home together.

"It must've been about ten minutes. No more than that, and she was gone!" Trish's voice cracked and her fear became audible. "I've looked everywhere in and around the house. She's not here."

"I'm calling the police," Nora said. "I'm also calling Jimmy at work. Maybe he and a couple of firefighters can check the neighborhood, but I'm so afraid, you know, after what happened to her."

Sergeant Andrews heard the anxiousness in Nora's voice. A cold prickly feeling crawled across the skin on his scalp.

"Please help us! We've got to find her!"

"I'm on my way." He disconnected and hurried along the hall to the dispatch station. His mind raced. There was not much crime in the near west neighborhood, Jefferson, where the Noble's lived, but he didn't want to take any chances. He motioned to two officers who put down their coffee cups and ran toward him.

Andrews told the dispatcher, "I'm taking two cars with me over to the Jefferson district to look for a missing child."

The dispatcher's eyes grew wide. "Yes, sir. What can I do?"

"Put out an APB on an eight-year-old girl, white, dark hair. I don't know what she was wearing yet. Last seen in the Jefferson neighborhood. I'm not taking any chances this time."

"Roger that," Sally said. "Sergeant, do we know anything else about her?"

"Yes," Andrews said over his shoulder as he rushed away. "Her name is Grace Richards, but she goes by Amy Jericho."

Sylvia's heart vaulted inside her chest. Surely this was part of the Gilliver curse, and now her niece was prey to it–again.

She sat holding the cordless phone after disconnecting, staring at the late afternoon beauty of an early fall day from her bedroom veranda. The clandestine caller told her the police had been dispatched to look for a missing child. Amy Jericho. Grace!

Sylvia shook her head to chase away the worst thoughts flooding her mind. Abduction. Danger. Kidnapping. Perhaps, she told herself, Grace was playing with a neighbor child and somehow her foster mother didn't know about it. *But how could that be?*

In a blind terror, she jumped up, grabbed her car keys and ran downstairs, stopping only to retrieve a flashlight from the kitchen. She almost bumped into Marianna, who stood chopping vegetables, as she spun on her heel to sprint outside.

Once in her car, driving away, Sylvia began to calm her thinking. *What could she do that the police weren't doing? Well, at least she could be another pair of eyes.* She was unfamiliar with the Jefferson district where she knew Grace had been staying, so she drove first around the streets of her own neighborhood, fearing every shadow, remembering the worst. But the manicured landscaping seemed perfectly in place in the changing light of the day's end.

Then, her thoughts bolted. She knew someone Grace may have wanted to see. Making an abrupt U-turn, she sped through angled streets of the west side bluffs toward the river. The light was fading as she parked in front of Mercer's store, now closed, across from the fateful railroad crossing. Walking briskly across the street, she paused at the tracks. *This is where it all began.*

Beyond the tracks, she could see the shadowy hulks of earth moving machinery. The houses were gone. Sylvia swallowed the bitter taste rising in her mouth because of Brian's land scheme. *What happened to the people who lived there? Brian probably never considered them.*

In the faintly lit backdrop, a tiny figure could be seen huddled on what looked like cement steps. It was the only part left of a once proud house, a house filled with love.

Sylvia switched on the flashlight and began to run toward the silhouette calling, "Grace! Grace!" The figure moved but as she got closer, it turned its back toward her.

Panting, Sylvia stopped a few steps away. Her relief turned to somber pity. This child had been through so much. She knelt in the muddy ground next to the disembodied steps and stretched her hand to touch the girl's shoulder.

"Grace," she whispered. "Grace, I've found you."

Sylvia knew from the angle of her trembling shoulders Grace was crying. She searched her mind for something to say to comfort her. She tried again. "Grace, you don't have to be afraid anymore. Come with me, please, Grace."

The girl's head snapped around then, and those guileless grey eyes, so like her own, searched Sylvia's face for a moment before she said in a loud, clear voice, "My name is Amy."

EPILOGUE

Final Grace

Fourteen Years Later

Charlie pounced on the ringing phone.

"Are you ready?" Sylvia asked.

"Sure, yes, I guess so." He tamped down the fluttering feeling rising in him.

"I'm getting close to the exit to Tillman now. I left Dan and the two boys sleeping because I wanted to be sure to get there early. It's been an easy drive from Atlanta at this time of the day."

Half an hour later they were on the road to a small private college nestled in the rolling hills of eastern Tennessee, Sylvia's alma mater. Neither spoke much, preferring the silence to nurture their own thoughts in the splendid freshness of early morning May in Tennessee. A fine day for a graduation.

Now stooped and bent, Leland met them at the back of the rows of vivid white painted folding chairs. His white bushy eyebrows seemed grown together, but he still exuded a confident power as he stopped to greet people he knew. He clapped Charlie on the back as he shook his hand. "Guess we're all getting older. Wonder where our girl is?" he said, looking around.

They made their way toward the front of the seats, acknowledging people they knew along the way. The sharp green of the late spring grass touched the steady blue of the sky on the hilltop horizon. Brick buildings with white-washed trim that comprised the tiny campus seemed to glow in the sunshine.

After they settled into their seats and glanced over the programs, Sylvia said, "Our girl is graduating at the head of her class. What a proud moment."

"The only thing missing," Charlie said, "is that Mae isn't here to see her." All three of them became thoughtful while the chairs filled with other guests.

The graduates tittered around in their robes, greeting friends and family, sharing nervous and excited chatter.

Sylvia spotted her first. "There's Grace," she said, pointing to a slender young woman with shiny dark hair. Though none of them had seen her for fourteen years, there was no mistaking her. She was with a group of other graduates milling through the crowd.

She passed by so closely Charlie could almost reach out to touch her. She paused and looked directly at him with those huge inquiring grey eyes. For a moment, there was a flicker of recognition, and then she was swept away with her friends.

Purple clouds hugged the horizon displaying sheets of stars in the dark ether above. As Charlie walked out of his new house, a train whistled in the distance, and he remembered.

End

ACKNOWLEDGEMENTS

The idea for this book came to me in Pomona, Illinois, while I was visiting my brother and sister-in-law during a "writing retreat" week they graciously hosted for me each winter for some years. My appreciation to my brother, Rick Williams, and beautiful sister-in-law, Theresa Lusch. They continue to support and encourage my writing efforts.

I've had some wonderful beta readers who took the time to both read my drafts and respond with helpful, detailed comments and feedback. This book is better thanks to them. Special thanks to Gayla Betts, Vicki Miller, Don Mead, Melanie Faith, Deborah Corker, Molly Edwards-Britton and the Saluki Writer's Group including but not limited to Ryan Crawford, Andrew Swearingen, Sandra Sidi, Cole Buccia, Jennifer and Sequoia.

I've been fortunate to attend writing workshops conducted by Bart Yates and Adam Johnson during which parts of this work were discussed and critiqued. It has, no doubt, become much better because of them.

Judge Souk in McLean County, Illinois, and Ronda Glenn helped with the legal questions I had, and Robyn Cashen provided information about the workings of DCFS and Shelter Care hearings. Glenn Wright explained about guns and hunting. I am so, so grateful to all of them.

Finally, I want to thank my wonderful husband, David Armstrong, for his consistency, understanding and all the goodness we have in our marriage.